Lee Bonds

PublishAmerica
Baltimore

First printing

At the specific preference of the author, PublishAmerica allowed this work to remain exactly as the author intended, verbatim, without editorial input.

ISBN: 1-4241-2271-6
PUBLISHED BY PUBLISHAMERICA, LLLP
www.publishamerica.com
Baltimore

Printed in the United States of America

To Bill
Good Luck & Best Wishes
Thank you for reading
my Book

Lee Bond

I would like to dedicate this book to my wife Charlotte who encouraged and helped me stay focused when I lost my way. She believed in me when others didn't. Thank you my darling

Jace McCord woke from a fitful sleep. He couldn't remember where he was. His head hurt and he was sick deep inside. Slowly, his memory began to return. He started to remember how he had come home from a couple of days rounding up cattle on his ranch and found his wife and baby daughter dead in the cabin. Jace had a hard time trying to remember that time. There was so much pain. He remembered how he came to himself after a couple of days and had to bury them. Then he remembered the hate for those who did this and how he vowed to track them down.

He spent weeks trying to find out who had taken his life away from him and plotted how he would take revenge. But he couldn't find any clues to those who had done this horrible thing. The only thing he knew was that whoever had killed his family had taken Karen's ring and necklace, something he had especially made for her on a trip to San Francisco. The ring and necklace were one of a kind. If he found the person or persons who had them, he would find the killers.

Jace had spent almost a year drunk, trying to stop the horrible nightmares. But they still came at night and troubled his restless sleep. He spent long lonely days and nights trying to make sense of what had happened to him and why it had happened. Jace wandered from place to place, cleaning stables and bars; anything that would buy him another bottle and something to eat. Finally, he knew something had to happen to turn his life around; otherwise, he would die, and he knew that wasn't what Karen would want for him. Once, Jace had even thought about doing something to himself to stop the pain, but he knew he couldn't do that. He had to do something soon, or else the whiskey would kill him.

Jace walked from the alley where he had slept and suddenly remembered he'd had nothing to eat for a long time. He couldn't remember how long it had been, but he was so hungry that he was weak and couldn't think clearly. Passing a storefront window, he caught his reflection in the window and didn't like what he saw. He was dirty, his clothes were in rags, and he had not shaven in he could not remember how long. All of a sudden he was brought out of his thoughts by a woman's scream. He ran toward the sound and found three men in an alley. They were tearing a young woman's clothes and pushing her from one to the other, making dirty remarks about her. Jace didn't know what to do. He had no weapon, and he was so weak from hunger that he couldn't take on all three of them. However, he knew he had to do something. As Jace entered the alley, he noticed a man ahead of him with a gun in his holster. Easing up beside the man, he slipped the gun out and stuck it in his own belt. Jace moved closer and spoke threateningly, "Leave the girl alone!"

The three men stopped and looked at him. One of the men spoke to the hard case holding the girl.

"Well, Red, what do you think this bastard wants?"

Red laughed. "Maybe he thinks he can take us all three."

All three of the men laughed. Jace didn't like the fact that they were hurting the girl, and he didn't like being laughed at.

He thought back to a time when they wouldn't have laughed at him.

"Leave her alone!"

They laughed again.

"What are you going to do about it if we don't?" Red snarled.

Jace didn't say anything. The cold look in his eyes should have been enough to warn them, but they were too busy laughing at him.

Red spoke again. "I see you have a gun. You want to take all three of us on?"

"I don't see a problem with that. I've faced better than you three."

"Okay, mister. Anytime you're ready." He pushed the girl aside and told his two friends to spread out, warning the crowd that had gathered around not to butt into their business. What happened next was something the town talked about for a long time. The three men reached for their pistols and had just cleared leather when three rapid shots rang out. The three men lay on the ground dead. The hushed crowd began to whisper about what had happened. They hadn't even see the stranger move; yet, all of a sudden he had a gun in his hand and the three men lay dead.

Jace stood, trying to get a focus on reality. Eventually, he noticed the girl with an elderly man holding her up. Through her sobs, the girl told the man how this stranger had saved her life. The man and the girl came to Jace. The old man spoke, "Young man is there anything we can do for you?"

Jace was still trying to get a focus on reality when he answered with, "I don't understand?"

"My name's Fred Lawson, This is my daughter Jennifer that you saved. I'd like to repay that."

"Those men didn't need to be pushing other people around."

Just then a man with a star on his shirt came up." What's goin' on here?" he asked.

After the crowd told him what had happened, the sheriff spoke directly to Jace.

"Mister, let me have your gun until I can get this straightened out."

The older man spoke up immediately. "Ben, this man just saved Jennifer's life. That's the reason those three men are there on the street."

"Well, Fred, if you say he's okay, I guess it's all right."

Then Ben spoke to Jace again, "Stranger, what's your name."

"Jason McCord."

"You the one they call The Shooter?"

"I haven't been called that in a long time."

The sheriff gasped, "Sorry, Mr. McCord. I didn't know."

Fred stepped closer, "Now, Ben, aren't you glad you didn't try to take his gun?"

Fred then turned to speak to Jace. "Mr. McCord, I need to talk to you later about the shooting."

"Anytime."

The sheriff interjected, "Sure, Ben, but I need to talk to him, too."

"Look, Ben, I need to talk to him now. Can he come to your office later?"

The sheriff agreed. Jace followed Fred and Jennifer to an office. The sign on the front of the building read 'Fred Lawson, Attorney at Law'. When the trio entered the office, Fred pointed to a chair and said, "Have a seat, Mr. McCord. Let's talk about what I can do to repay you for my daughter's life."

"Mr. Lawson, I don't want payment for saving your daughter's life. I just couldn't stand by and let them hurt her."

"You could have, and most people in this town would have. There must be something I can do for you."

Jace thought for a minute and then responded, "Well, I haven't eaten in a while. If you could give me enough money to get a bite of food, I'd appreciate it."

Jennifer spoke for the first time, "We can do more than that, can't we daddy?"

Ben turned to his daughter, "Go to the Delta House. Get Jace a room and make arrangements for a bath. Then go to the Mercantile and tell Harry to set up an account for Jason McCord. Tell him that he'll be over soon to get some new clothes."

Jennifer nodded and left.

"Mr. McCord, I don't mean to be so nosy, but how did you get in the shape you're in? Most everyone has heard your name, so something has happened to get you this far down."

"Please call me Jace."

"Okay, I'm Fred."

"Fred, I really can't talk about my problems right now, but maybe someday we can talk and I can tell you more about them."

The two men talked for a while before Jennifer came back. When she came in the door, Jennifer said, "Father, I'm going to take Mr. McCord to the Mercantile and help him pick out some clothes and see that he's treated right at the hotel. We'll meet you at the Cattleman's Club for dinner." Then she turned and spoke softly to Jace, "Mr. McCord, please come with me."

Jace agreed to go with her if she'd call him by his name, not "Mr. McCord."

Jennifer blushed, nodded in agreement, and they left. While they were walking, Jennifer questioned Jace, "Why do people call you The Shooter?"

"I don't like that name. I got it because so many men wanted to try me out. I've had to shoot a lot of men I didn't want to because they were trying to kill me."

After buying a few clothes at the Mercantile, Jennifer escorted Jace the hotel and waited while he bathed and changed. When Jace decended the stairs, Jennifer met him with a smile and said, "Let's go eat."

Jace and Jennifer met Fred and another girl at the Cattleman's Club restaurant. Jace noticed that the other girl looked a lot like Jennifer, except she had a reddish color hair. "Jace, I'd like for you to meet my other daughter Jessica."

"Happy to meet you."

Fred invited everyone to sit down and order. He said, "You sure look different in those clothes, Jace."

"Thanks, I feel better and I appreciate this, too."

Jace ordered steak, potatoes, and lots of hot coffee. It had been so long since he'd eaten, he didn't think he could get enough, He remembered times when he would have given anything for a meal like this. There were times when he felt like he might starve. He filled up sooner than he thought he would.

After the meal, Fred spoke to Jace.

"How about coming to meet with me tomorrow, Jace? I've got a job prospect I'd like to talk to you about."

"Thanks, I could sure use a way to make some money."

Fred excused himself saying that he had a busy day coming up.

Jennifer gazed across the table at Jace and said, "Jace, would you like to walk down to the river and talk for a little while?"

Jace nodded and said, "That'd be nice."

"Don't be late getting home," Fred warned them, "although I expect you're in very safe company."

As he left the restaurant with Jennifer, Jace bid Fred and Jessica goodnight.

Jennifer and Jace walked silently for a while before she broke the silence. "Jace, you ever been married . . . or do you have a girlfriend?"

Jace paused a beat before he answered her. "I was married once."

"What happened?"

"I can't talk about it right now; it's too hard to think about. But, if I ever feel like talking about it, you're the one I'd talk to."

Jace looked at Jennifer, admiring her beauty. She had long blonde hair and the prettiest blue eyes he had ever seen. She was wearing a beautiful pink dress that moved smoothly across her beautiful body as she walked. Jace liked looking at her.

"I've never felt so safe with anyone else. When those men were hurting me and you came into the alley, I saw something in you that was more than just a man dressed in old clothes."

Jace smiled. "Well, the last couple of years have been pretty rough."

"I can't tell you how I felt when you told them to leave me alone. It was like every thing was going to be all right even though you were alone and facing three men. You had an air about you that told me you would take care of me, and I would be safe."

The two talked and walked for quite a while. Jace found himself enjoying his time with her. He had not felt like this with anyone else since his wife had been killed. With Jennifer, talking was so easy for him, and he felt relaxed. Jennifer related how much she missed her mother, and how good her father had been to her. But, she secretly wished her mother was still around to teach her things she needed to know about courtship and men.

"I think I should walk you home now. It is getting cool and I don't want your father to worry about you."

"I haven't enjoyed an evening like this ever before. I enjoy talking to you and you seem so gentle. I don't see how all the stories about you could be true."

"I have enjoyed tonight, too, but it will take a little time to get past my old memories and hurts. All the stories you hear are not true. I have lived a very hard life and had to kill men I didn't want to. Jennifer, I would like to see you again sometime"

"I would like that, too," she replied. "Good night."

Jennifer woke with a smile, remembering the wonderful man she had met. She thought of his bronzed features, his good looks, his broad shoulders, his dark hair and his moustache. He was the kind of man that made her feel so safe. Smiling to herself, she thought, "This is the kind of man I always wanted to meet." She liked tall men, and Jace was over 6 feet tall. She found it hard to get him out of her mind; this incredible man who had saved her from a horrible fate.

The next morning Jace met with Fred in his office. Fred greeted him with a jolly "Good morning, Jace, how was your night?"

"It's the best night I've had in a long time. I can't remember sleeping that well for quite a while. I don't usually sleep so sound. I have to be alert all the time. People are trying to kill me anyway they can, just to say they killed the shooter."

"Well, I guess it is pretty bad, being in your shoes. I have never had to live like that. I don't know how it would be."Shifting in his chair, Fred continued, "The reason I wanted to talk to you was that we had two men come into town a while back. They killed three people in cold blood. We just found out they are in Yuma prison. We want them brought back to stand trial for the murder of our citizens. I have contacted the Yuma prison and made arrangements to have them brought here. This is where you come in. I want you to bring them home for us."

Jace thought for a while and said, "I don't think I can bring them both back by myself."

Fred laughed and said, "You can hire all the help you need to bring them home. We trust your judgment and your ability to do the job."

Jace stood up and looked out the window for a while before answering. "I'd like to travel to Yuma by horse. That would give me some time to think about all I have been through this past couple of years."

Fred nodded his head understandinigly, "That would be just fine, as long as we get them back home to stand trial."

Just then, Ben the sheriff came running into Fred's office. In his hand was a poster he had found. Jace was still there when Ben burst in the door. Ben looked at Jace when he spoke.

"Remember the two men I told you about?"

Jace nodded.

"They're wanted for murder and robbery in Texas."

"What could they want in Kansas?" Fred asked.

"Don't know, but whatever it is, Jace needs to watch his back."

Jace stood to go, "Well I had better get going, I will need a few supplies."

Fred followed Jace to the door, "I've made arrangements at the livery for a horse and saddle. You can get anything else you need at the mercantile."

Ben told Jace, "Come by the office. I've got the guns I took off the three men you shot.They might come in handy."

"Thanks, I'll stop by after while to pick them up."

At the livery stable, Jace chose a good, strong horse that looked like it could take the long hard trip ahead. As he was saddling the horse, Jennifer came into the livery.

"Father' told me what you are going to do," Jennifer confided. "Please be careful. Come back safe."

Jace thought a minute before turning to look at Jennifer. "I find myself thinking about you a lot. I'll come back. That's a promise."

Jennifer stood in front of him, raised herself on her tiptoes, and gave Jace a kiss. "Please hurry back."

Jace felt her warm breath on his lips and couldn't remember anything as soft and gentle as her kiss.

"I'll be back before you know it."

It was noon before he was ready to leave. He told Ben, "I think I'll get something to eat before I leave."

"Yeah, sometimes you don't get much to eat on the trail," Ben remarked.

"I've eaten more than one meal in the saddle, "Jace replied.

"I'll see you when you get back, Jace."

"Take care of things while I am gone."

It felt good to be in the saddle again. Jace rode until dark and looked for a good place to make camp. Noticing a good stand of oak trees nearby, Jace headed towared them. He was rewarded with finding a stream nearby, too. Jace reined in his horse and started to set up camp. He took the saddle and pack off the horses. He hobbled them and let them graze on an abundance of lush green grass. It took a while, but Jace finally gathered enough wood to start a good fire and get the coffee on.

After relishing his beans and hot coffee, Jace's thoughts turned to Jennifer. She was so beautiful, and being close to her made him feel good. He had never met anyone quite like her. The only sound was the breeze in the trees. He felt focused and in control of his life again. The pain was still there,

but it didn't hurt as much. Just then a squirrel started his chatter. Jace drifted off to sleep. He woke refreshed and feeling good. After he ate and had his coffee, he saddled the horses and continued on his journey.

As he had done for so long, Jace let his mind wander to the painful past. Suddenly, a vision of Jennifer came to his mind. Thinking of her brought a smile to his face. She was exquisitely beautiful and everything a man could want. Jace knew he had no chance with her, however. He was a gunfighter turned drunk. He had nothing to offer her. Jennifer deserved a man without a sordid past; a man with money who could provide her with a fine home and lovely things. Neverless, Jace thought about her a lot that day.

As he rode, Jace thought about his life and what brought him to this place. Growing up with his father and mother and a brother and sister had been a very happy existence until the war. Jace and his brother were taken to fight, and he had not seen his family since. A soldier at sixteen, Jace was scared all the time. He saw men killed for the first time in his life, and he thought he wouldn't be able to stand it. Once after an especially bloody day on the battlefield, Jace was literally shaking in his boots. An old, seasoned soldier took pity on the young boy and took him under his wing. The old man taught Jace many things about life, death, and war. The old soldier also told Jace that he must learn to shoot fast and straight in order to save his life. It was kill or be killed.

One day after a battle, Jace found a gun and holster. Taking the old man's advice, he strapped it on and started shooting every spare minute. All of the men in his company encouraged young Jace and were soon talking about how fast and accurate his shooting was becoming. During one battle his old friend was killed. That was the first time Jace had faced the death of someone close to him. After that experience, he pulled away from everyone in his company. Jace didn't want to lose anyone else close to him. He practiced shooting more and more, getting faster and more accurate with each day.

After the war, Jace went home and found the old home place burned, and everyone gone. He learned from neighbors that his parents had been killed and his sister taken away, possibly by enemy soldiers. His brother never came home from the war. There was nothing to stay near for.

Jace found a horse wandering near his burned out home. He straddled the horse and just started drifting. Men soon found out he was good with a gun and wanted the challenge of facing him in a gunfight. They wouldn't leave him alone. Although he tried to avoid these face offs, men hounded him constantly. Jace was forced to kill when he didn't want to. He figured if he went a long way from his home maybe no one would know him.

His mind drifted back to the time when he met Karen. Jace found himself in northern New Mexico. It was spring and the grass was green and the weather cool. As he came over a hill, Jace spotted a beautiful valley with a house, a barn, and a bunkhouse. Cattle were grazing contendedly in the green pasture. A large stream flowed through the valley. It was a beautiful sight. Jace rode down to the house, and an older man came out to meet him. He said his name was Mark West. Jace got down off his horse and introduced himself.

Mark said, "Wouldn't be looking for a job, would you?"

"I sure could use one," Jace replied.

"Well, young feller come sit on the porch and let's talk."

While the two men were talking, a lovely, young woman came out of the house. She announced,

"Dad, lunch is ready. Oh, sorry. I didn't know you had company."

"Jace, this is my daughter Karen."

"Glad to meet you, "Jace said.

"Dad, lunch is ready. Maybe your friend would like to have lunch with us."

"Good idea. How 'bout it, Jace?"

"I don't want to put you to any trouble Miss Karen,"

"No trouble. It's already on the table. I can set another place, and we're ready."

"Come on in and we can talk while we eat," Mark said.

When they were finished eating, Mark wanted to show Jace around. "We'll be back in a while honey."

"It was very nice to meet you, Mr. McCord," Karen said as the men walked out the door.

"Thank you and the name is Jace, not Mr. McCord.

Jace went to work for Mark West and was very happy. No one knew him in that part of the country. The men he worked with treated him like one of them. It felt good to be just a cowhand.

As time went by, Karen started seeking out opportunities to be around Jace. He liked the attention, and she was a good-looking young woman.

Once, while Jace was washing up for supper, Mark surprised him when he said, "Karen is quit taken with you."

"I think she is a very wonderful girl, too, Mark. I like being around her," Jace replied. Jace understood that Mark was giving his permission for Jace to court Karen. He was eager to do so.

After a few months Jace and Karen were married and later had a baby. Mark West thought highly of Jace and was delighted when he became a grandpa. Mark told Jace that he would leave every thing he had to him and Karen. A few months later, Mark became very ill and died. Jace and Karen seemed lost without him. They had a hard time getting back to their lives again. Mark had been like a father to Jace.

One day Jace told Karen he had to go check the cattle in the hills before the snow came. As usual, she fixed him some food for the trip, kissed him,and said, "Please be careful."

Jace was gone four days, checking on the cattle. When he came in sight of the house, he was happy to be coming home to his wife and baby. However, something didn't seem right. Jace stopped his horse, dismounted quickly, and started on foot to the house. When he reached the house, his heart was in his throat. Something was very wrong; Karen should have come to meet him by now. He pulled his gun and kicked the door open. As he jumped through the door, what Jace saw almost made him pass out. His wife and baby lay dead on the floor. He fell down and gathered them into his arms. He didn't remember how long he lay there in grief and disbelief, but it had been a long time. Finally, Jace had the strength to take his wife and baby out and bury them beside her father. He sat by the graves a long time. The pain ripped him apart and was almost more than he could bear. Then, anger took over. Jace was in a rage; he would find and kill anyone who was responsible for this.

Jace spent three months trying to track the killers, but didn't find a clue as to who took his world away from him. He started drinking more and more, until he hardly remembered what he was looking for. He found himself in towns and didn't remember where he was. Many mornings, Jace woke up in some alley, and didn't know how he got there. He worked in barns cleaning stalls and in saloons cleaning floors and spittoons. Anything he could do to get enough for a drink and something to eat. His clothes hardly fit him for he had lost so much weight. Deep inside, Jace knew he must stop this, or he would kill himself. His thoughts returned to the day he met Jennifer. He thought how beautiful she was and how much he liked being around her. But he knew he was kidding himself. He was not in her class. She was a fine lady, and he was a fast gun with no way to take care of her.

At the end of his second day on the Yuma Trail, Jace camped

in a place with few trees. However, a good stream ran close by, and the horses again had plenty of lush green grass to graze on. It was a good place to make camp for the night. Jace had been a little uneasy all day. He had a feeling he was being followed that day. Although he didn't see anyone, he had a sixth sense about such things. He didn't see anyone on the trail; however, Jace had seen a plume of dust in the distance. It might be nothing, but he had lived this long by trusting his instincts.

After tending to the horses, Jace made camp and started a fire and cooked some bacon, beans, and coffee. He built the fire up and put his saddle down. Next, Jace put his role under his blanket with his hat on top to look like he was asleep. He moved to the top of a rise and lay down to wait. As he lay back on a big rock almost ready to doze off, he heard a sound. Suddenly, Jace became alert and listened close for anything that was not a normal night sound. The moon rose above the horizon, and Jace heard something. He looked hard into the night trying to make out anything there in the dark. Suddenly, he saw it—two men crawling on the ground. They moved slowly toward his camp. As they neared his bedroll, one of the men whispered to the other one, "We've got him. The men stood up and cut loose the bed roll.

"Well, you boys missed me," Jace hollered into the night. The two men were taken by surprise and turned to fire at Jace. But he shot first. He hit the first one in the chest and the second man in the shoulder. The wounded man tried to shoot Jace again. Jace wanted to take him alive, but he had to fire fast and he hit the man between the eyes. Both lay dead, their lifeblood leaking out in the dry sand. Jace decided to turn one of their horses loose and keep one for a pack horse. The two men had several things Jace could use, so he would need the extra horse. Jace found a Spencer rifle and a Colt revolver as he rumanged through the dead men's packs. He had heard about the Spencer rifle. It could fire 16 times before reloading; this was the first one Jace had ever seen. He was just about to bury them when he noticed an Arkansas toothpick in one on the men's boot. He unrolled a bed roll and found a two gun rig. That would come in very handy he thought.

Jace got an early start the next morning. He knew it would be a long day, but he hoped to be a lot closer to Yuma by night fall. Lulled by the warming sun, Jace's mind returned to pleasant thoughts of Jennifer. Suddenly, Jace straigtened up in his saddle as he noticed hoof prints of seven or eight horses moving in the same direction he was. He noticed not all the horses carried riders because some of the prints were not as deep as others. This country could be could be wild with outlaws running through it regularly. However, these ponies were unshod and that meant Indians. The Pumas were in this country and maybe they would not bother him. However, this was also Apache territory, and Jace didn't want to meet up with them. He got down and checked the tracks. They were fresh and still had morning moisture around the edge. They could not be over a couple of hours ahead of him.

He was in hilly country and had just come to a long flat stretch of land. There was a mountain range, but he had to cross the flat land before he reached the mountains. Jace thought for a while, figuring out the best way to cross the flats without being spotted by the Indians. He decided to cross at night; therefore, he made a cold camp, had some jerky and water, and slept until sundown. He saddled his horse and packhorse and waited until it was dark before starting out. He reached the mountains about midnight where he found a hole in some rocks that led to a canyon. Jace could leave his horses there while he scouted around. The time he spent with the Comanche Indians would come in handy right now. He left the horses and climbed to a high point to see what was ahead of him. He spotted a very faint glow past one of the peaks and cautiously made his way to the top of that peak to check out the surroundings. Below him he spotted the Indians, camping for the night. They must have had some whiskey to drink because they had made a bigger fire than usual. Jace couldn't hear them, so he settled down and waited until they were asleep. Why were they here? These Indians didn't have any war paint on. Could they be hunting this far from their home? He remembered hearing that the land had been very dry for this time of year. Maybe the game had gone off for water, and the Indians were forced to hunt out this far. Because he would probably be there for a while, Jace made himself comfortable and slept. When he woke, the Indians were loading three deer and some smaller game on to the extra horses pack horses. Jace sighed with relief, knowing the Indians would soon start home and he could be on his way again. After they were gone, Jace waited a while before he left, putting distance between him and the Indians.

Remembering that this mountain range had the last good water he would find for a while, Jace decided to spent the night at a river. He took care of the horses and hobbled them so they could drink and graze on the lush grass along the river. They would not get such a good chance on the rest of their trip. As soon as the horses were taken care of, he took off his clothes and enjoyed a refreshing swim in the river. Afterwards, Jace washed his clothes and hung them to dry. He prepared a good meal, put a blanket by his saddle, and rested for a while. He slept fitfully, knowing that like an animal, anything unusual would wake him.

Jace woke refreshed the next morning. The horses, too, were in good shape for the long hard trip ahead. He did not see any new tracks for now, so he rode relaxed, thinking about his past and what had brought him to this place. Jennifer occupied much, of his thoughts and that was very pleasant. He had ridden for two days with everything well, except for the lack of water. Occasionally, Jace had found some pools of water; but, they were few and far between. On the fifth day he grew more concerned because he had not found more water. The horses were beginning to show signs of wear. Taking off his hat, he poured some water into it from his last canteen and gave the horse a drink. Jace hoped he could find water soon. He didn't know how much longer he or the horses could go without water.

Jace's mouth was as dry as a desert and his body felt parched from the sun beating down upon him. He didn't know if he was even thinking right. He knew he needed water soon. Gazing into the distance, Jace thought he saw something ahead. But maybe it was just a mirage. As he rode, Jace watched it came into view. It was a cactus, and he remembered some held water. He spurred his horse to go more quickly. When he reached the cactus, Jace slid from his horse, grabbed his Arkansas toothpick from his boot, and put a cloth around his hand to protect him from the long thorns. He then cut into the cactus, reached inside, and took the pulp, and squeezed it into his parched mouth. Although it didn't taste very good, at least it was wet. He had a large pan he carried with him, and he put enough of the cactus flesh in the pan for his horses. At first, they didn't want to drink it, but their thirst over took the taste. They greedily drank the cactus water. Jace fed the horses the last of the feed and ate some jerky himself. Satisfied for awhile, they moved on.

Hopefully, two or three more days would get him to some country that had water, where he and the horses could rest. He focused on what he had to do: pick up two prisoners at Yuma and take them back to jail in Kansas. Jace needed to find two or three good men to help him on the return trip. It worried him where could he find men he could depend on. Good, dependable men could mean the difference between life and death for him. Maybe when he got to Yuma he could talk to the sheriff and get some help there.

The hot the sun beat down fiercely again, and the horses looked like they couldn't go much longer. He was riding and thinking when his horse stopped and perked up her ears and whinnied. Jace had learned to trust his horse when she felt trouble. Looking ahead, he saw a grove of trees in the distance and decided to circle around to see what had troubled his horse. It took most of the rest of the day to reach the trees since he had taken the long way around. About sundown, Jace came into the trees and rode into them looking for water. He decided to scout ahead on foot. He was about to give up when he saw a glow ahead. He used the things he learned when he lived with the Indians. He moved slowly ahead until he was close enough he could hear the men talking. He got on his belly and moved ahead until he was close enough to hear what was being said. One of the men said, "How long are we going to wait here?"

"Well, he should be here soon if he didn't get killed and save us the trouble." There were four men, and they were after someone. Jace wondered who they wanted and why.

One of the men said, "Why did we have to come two days from Yuma to do this? Why couldn't we just catch him outside town and gun him down?"

The man that seemed to be in charge said, "You don't just go up against a man like Jace McCord."

"Yeah, but there's four of us and only one of him."

One of the other men said, "Just leave to him to me and I will take care of him!"

"Yeah, and we will be diggin' your grave real soon."

Jace thought he was hearing things. Why would anyone want him dead? Well, there it was: these men were looking for him and wanted to kill him. He backed out of their range and walked back to his horses and tried to think of a plan. He decided the best thing to do was meet this thing head on. One of the men he had shot on the trail had a two-gun rig, which Jace had brought with him. He took it from his pack saddle and put it on. He was not much of a two-gun rig man, but it seemed like this was a time that it would come in handy. He practiced for hours until he noticed it was getting daylight.

Jace tended his horses and walked back to the camp where the four men were. When he got close, he started moving very lightly until he was just around a tree from them. Slipping around the tree, Jace said, "I heard you are looking for me!"

One of the men shouted, "Oh, shit! I can't believe this." They all turned to face Jace who was like a spring ready to uncoil.

The leader said, "Are you Jace McCord?"

"I sure am and I am here to find out why you are looking for me."

"We plan to kill you. Anything else you need to know while you are still breathing?" They all laughed.

Jace didn't say any more; he just watched the leader's eyes. He figured he would be the first one to make a move. Jace saw him start his move.Three shots from Jace's gun found their marks, but one man mananged to squeeze off a bullet that hit Jace in the left arm just as he shot the last man. For a few minutes, Jace sat down and put a rag around his arm to stop the bleeding. Then he went to the river and got a drink. He looked through their things to see if he could find a reason for the men looking to kill him. He didn't find anything to identify them, but each man had a fifty-dollar gold piece. He took anything he could use, and turned their horses loose, and went back to his horses. Although his arm was hurting, Jace had to put it out of his mind. He knew someone else might be looking to kill him. Getting to Yuma fast was more important than ever. He rode all that day and into the night because he wanted to reach town the next day if possible. He made camp sometime past midnight, he figured. He got an early start the next morning and was in sight of Yuma by two that afternoon.

Jennifer woke and found herself thinking about the man that had saved her life. She found herself thinking of Jace more than she should but she could not help herself. She made breakfast for her father and herself.

Fred said, "Jennifer's what are you so deep in thought about?"

She suddenly heard her father's voice and came to the present.

"I am not thinking of anything father."

He laughed and said, "I'll bet I can guess and it won't take but one guess."

"He will be in danger while he is bringing the prisoners back"

"I think he will be all right. The way he handles a gun I think he will be just fine sweetheart. Don't worry."

She said, "Father, I really like him, and I don't want anything to happen to him."

"Jace will be back soon and everything would be just fine."

When he rode into Yuma, he stopped at the sheriff's office to tell him about the incident at the creek with the four men. When he opened the door, he saw a well-groomed man behind the desk with a badge on.

"Yes, can I help you? My name's is Rick Johnson, sheriff of Yuma."

"Sheriff, my name is Jace McCord.and I was ambushed about a day out of Yuma by four men. I killed them and wanted to report in with you."

"You mean you killed four men by yourself and only got one hit in the arm?"

"Well let's just say I was lucky."

"Not from what I hear if you are the one they call the shooter."

"Sheriff..."

"No," he interrupted. "Call me Rick."

"Well, Rick, I don't like the name shooter and have tried to live it down.But people just won't forget."

"I know what you mean. Just the same, you are a very famous man. By the way what are you doing in Yuma?"

"I am here to pick up two prisoners for Ben Anderson, sheriff of Hays Kansas."

"I'm sorry to talk so much. You look like you could use a doctor. Go to the Yuma hotel and get a room and I will send the doctor to check you out," Rick said.

"Thanks, Rick, I will see you after I rest up a while."

"Give me a call, and I will go have dinner with you."

"Okay, see you then."

Jace was resting in his room when he heard footsteps in the hall. He took his colt out, moved to the door and waited. There was a knock and Jace said, "Who is it?"

"Dr. Malloy," came the reply.

He opened the door and saw a man with a white coat and a bag in his hand. He said, "Come on in,Doc."

"Let me look at your arm," the doctor replied." Jace took off his shirt and the doc checked his arm. "It looks like the bullet went through without hitting a bone. I think we can fix you up good as new."

After the doc left, he cleaned up, went downstairs and checked with the man at the desk, "Where is a good place to eat?"

"The Claxton house is a good place," the clerk replied.

"Thanks," Jace told him and left. He walked to the sheriff's office and met Rick. They walked down the road to the Claxton house.

Rick said, "This is about as good a place to eat as we have in Yuma."

"Sounds good to me," replied Jace.

After they had a good meal Jace said, "I am tired, so if you don't mind I think I will turn in."

"Okay, see you in the morning," Rick told him.

Jace felt like could use a good night's sleep even if it was early. When he got back to his room, he undressed and got in bed. He couldn't sleep, however. What is these were not random things but were related. That meant someone was after him, but that couldn't't be. He had been adrunk the last two years. Why would anyone want to kill him now? He was thinking about that, when Jennifer drifted into his mind. He felt himself smile as he thought about her. She was the most beautiful person he had ever laid eyes on. She was a pleasant thought, and he had a warm feeling when he thought about her. He drifted off to sleep with her on his mind.

Suddenly his inner reflexes brought him awake, and he felt something was wrong. Men who live like Jace had learned to feel danger even when they were sleeping. He reached for his colt on the headboard. Just as he pulled it, the door to his room flew open. He rolled to the back side of the bed as several shots exploded into his bed, where he had been just a second ago. He rolled, fired, and heard someone yell from pain and another man was dragging himself out of the room. Jace jumped up and told the man to stop! He turned to fire at Jace. Jace had no choice but to shoot. He didn't't have time to place his shot. He wanted the man alive so he could find out why they were trying to kill him. However, the man groaned in pain and lay still. The sheriff,Rick Johnson, came running in and yelled, "What happened?"

Jace groaned, "I don't know, but they gave me a wake up call I guess."

Rick pleaded, "Please, this is no time for jokes."

"I know. I don't know why they were trying to kill me."

"Maybe they were in the wrong room," Rick thought out loud.

"I don't know but maybe the night clerk at the desk can tell us something. Just a minute while I get dressed." They went down stairs and found the night man. He looked like he was going to pass out any minute. Jace and Rick ask him about the two men that had come to Jace's room. His voice shaking, the night clerk told them that the two men came in, put a gun to his head, and ask where Jace McCord was. He told them." I am sorry Mr. McCord I didn't have any choice." "It's okay, "Jace answered. He knew the clerk had no choice.

"Rick, can we try to get some sleep now?"

The sheriff relented, "Okay, but meet me for breakfast in the morning. We can talk then."

As the sun broke over the horizon, Jace woke and was ready for breakfast. He went by the sheriff's office first. However, the deputy said that the sheriff would meet him at the café. When he walked in, Jace saw the sheriff sitting at a table with two men.

Rick said, "Jace, this is Fred Barlow and Hank Lassiter." Jace shook hands with them and sat down.

"I told both these men that you were going to take the

prisoners back and would need help. Barlow and Lassiter agreed to help," said Rick.

"Glad to have them along, but they need to know it will be a long dangerous trip. Someone has been trying to kill me, and I didn't know why."

Hank said, "We still want to go along."

"Well, I would be happy to have you along, but I just wanted you to know it is going to be dangerous. Ever since I left Kansas, someone has been trying to get me."

Hank said, "I still want to go."

"Me to," Fred replied.

After breakfast Jace went to the livery to see if he could get the horses he needed to take the prisoners to Santa Fe, where he could catch the train. He was able to get horses and equipment to make the trip. He thought about his trip to Yuma. He thought how thirsty he had been. He didn't't think a drink would hurt him, but only one. He went to the nearest saloon and ordered a beer. He was enjoying the drink when a man bumped into him.

Jace said, "Sorry."

The man said, "You sure are. Watch where you're going." Just then another man bumped him from behind. When Jace turned to face the man, the first man hit him and all of a sudden he was on the floor. At least three men and maybe more were hitting and kicking him. He didn't have a chance to get to his feet to fight back. He was about to pass out when he saw a giant pull the men off him, and slam them to the floor. That was the biggest man he had ever seen in his life. The giant reached down and pulled Jace to his feet. He was pretty shaky on his feet and still trying to clear his head when Rick Johnson walked in.

"What happened?" Rick asked

"I don't know. Three men or maybe more jumped me, and a giant pulled them off me."

Rick laughed, "Maybe in your condition you thought it was a giant. Jace, I would like for you to meet Luther Anderson."

He shook the biggest hand he ever seen. His shoulders looked like a plow horse and his arms like tree trunks.

"Well, Luke, I sure want to be one of your friends. I am afraid your enemies wouldn't be in to good a shape after tangling with you."

"Rick said you was going to take some prisoners to Kansas, and I sure would like to go with you," was Luke's reply.

"I'd like to have you with us, but it will be a long dangerous trip," Jace said. "Aw that's alright. I don't mind a little excitement once in a while," Luke replied.

"Well, Luke, I would really like to have you with us. Meet us in Fred's office in the morning."

"See you then," Luke smiled. "Jace, could you go to my office with me and talk?" Rick asked.

"Sure," Jace replied.

When they got to the sheriff's office Rick said, "Have a seat and I will fix some coffee."

When they were drinking their coffee Rick said," Jace, do you have any idea why the four men jumped you outside of town?"

"No, I don't and that has not been the first time either."

"Maybe you've made someone mad lately," ventured Rick.

"Well I guess any thing's possible. I found my wife and baby killed a little over a year ago. I have been drunk since then. I can't see someone wanting to kill me now. I don't think anyone even knows where I am now."

Rick said, "Maybe it was someone from before that."

"I can't think of anyone that would be looking for me for that long. I guess anything is possible."

"Well, be careful because someone is definitely trying to kill you."

"Can I talk to the prisoners before we take off?" Jace asked.

"Sure come on and I'll take you back there."

When they got to the cells, Hank yelled, "You better let us out if you know what is good for you sheriff!"

Rick laughed, "You better keep your mouth shut. This is the man that is going to take you back to Kansas to hang."

Bart said, " You're a dead man, mister. You better just mind your own business. You'll never get us back to Hays while you are still alive."

Jace said, "Rick, you didn't tell me they were so talkative. Maybe when they get to trial they'll be able to tell everyone why they murdered the men in Kansas."

Jace left the office and went to his room to rest for awhile. He thought about the trip ahead and decided they needed a couple extra men to help them reach Santa Fe and the train. He felt like after they reached the train, four of them could make the rest of the trip with the prisoners. After he rested for a while, he went to Rick and ask if he knew a couple of men they could use to get to Santa Fe.

"Talk to Fred Barlow. I think he can fix you up with a couple of good men," Rick replied.

Jace was getting hungry,so he went to the restaurant to get some lunch.

Fred and Hank were there, so he sat down at their table. After ordering something, Jace asked if they knew of anyone else to help them with the prisoners.

"I know a couple of men that might be interested. I could talk to them," Fred said. "They are good men that you could depend on and will follow orders."

"Why do you think we'll need more men?" Hank asked.

"Well, I have had several attempts on my life since I left Kansas. I think who ever is doing it won't stop. Maybe you two should think about the danger you'll be in," Jace told him.

"Well, we talked it over and we want to go. Do you think the men trying to kill you have anything to do with taking the prisoners to hang?" Fred asked.

"I don't see any reason someone would care about those two. They are just a couple of hard case that just wandered into town and killed a couple of men."

Hank asked, "When do you want to leave?"

"Get the two men ready,and we will all meet at the sheriff's office at eight in the morning. Be ready to start on the trip then."

Jace left the café and was headed to the livery to make sure the horses would be ready by morning. He saw Luke, "Are you in a big hurry?"

"No,"Jace said. "We can talk on the bench by the livery. What's on your mind, Luke?"

"Well, Mr. McCord...I mean Jace I have always been big,and I think people are afraid of me. Any way no one ever wants to let me help them or join in anything with them."

Jace said, "We will be leaving at eight in the morning. We will be very happy to have you with us."

"Thanks, mister...I mean, Jace. I'll be there. I've been looking forward to this."

He asked Luke, "Will you tell the others to meet me at the café in the morning? I'll buy breakfast.

Jennifer walked into her father'' office. "Have you heard anything about Jace?"

He said, "Yes, they are going to leave Yuma first thing in the morning."

"Do you think he will be in danger?" Jennifer ask her father.

"I don't see why they would be in to much danger. He has five men lined up to help him to Santa Fe. Then four of them will take the prisoners on the train the rest of the way."

"Father, I am worried about him, I like him and want him back here safe."

"Honey, don't worry, I don't see any problems;they are just bringing back a couple of saddle tramps for murder."

Jessica walked in and said, "Jen,will you help me pick out a new dress?"

"Sure I will be happy to help you," Jennifer replied.

Jessica said, "What are you looking so sad about?"

"I am so worried about Jace, although father said he didn't think I should worry. But I just have this feeling he is not safe. I just know he is in great danger."

Jessica said, "If father said not to worry,I don't think you should be afraid."

"I know Jess, but I care very much for him."

"I know; it's not hard to tell. You just light up when you talk about him."

They laughed and Jennifer said, "I just want him to come back to me safe and not hurt."

Jace was in the café the next morning when Fred and Hank walked in and sat down. After they all ordered breakfast, they talked about the trip. They stopped briefly when Luke came in to order, but picked up their conversation quickly. All of the men wondered what they might be in for on the long trip to Kansas. While they were talking two men walked in, and come to their table.

Hank said, "Jace these are the two men I was telling you about, Jim Taylor and Les Johnson. They said they would like to go with us to Santa Fe."

Jace said, "Glad to meet you. Pull up a couple of chairs and join us. Did Hank tell you there may be some danger involved in our trip?"

"Yeah, he told us, but we still want to go," Jim answered.

After they finished breakfast, Jace said he would meet them all at the sheriff's office as soon as he got everything ready. He went to the livery and the man had everything ready, just as Jace had requested. Jace thanked the man and gave him some extra money for the good job he had done. When he got to the sheriff's office, everyone was ready to go.

Jace said, "Everyone ready to go?"

"Yeah, we're ready," Luther told him.

"Rick, could you bring out the prisoners?"

As Rick brought the prisoners out Bart said, "You aren't going to get back alive. We have friends that will get us out of here."

Jace said, "I don't think you have any friends. But in case you do, they won't be very healthy if they try to break you loose. Now shut up and get on your horses!"When they were in the saddle he handcuffed them to the saddle horn and ran leg shackles under the horse to each foot.

Bart said, "What if our horse trips? We could be killed."

"Well, we'll have us a good cry," Luther laughed.

"If I was you, I'd be careful where my horse stepped," Jace answered. "If everyone is ready, let's get going."

They all told Rick bye and were on their way.

They started down the street toward the edge of town and on their trip.

Three men watched them leave and one said, "We better get the rest of the boys and get going if we are going to get ahead of them."

Lem said, "Let's get going, and we'll pick up the rest of our bunch at the edge of town. They should be ready to go so all we have to do is swing around and get in front of them and set up our ambush."

"Hank and Burt said they would slow them down as much as possible without getting too much attention. We should be ready to hit them day after tomorrow, if everything goes right.

Let' get going and hope Sam and the rest are ready to go."As they reached the edge of town, they saw Jace and his group heading out of town toward Santa Fe. They met Sam and his crew who were also ready to go. They set out to get ahead of Jace and his men.

Jace said, "What is the matter with you, Bart. You had better keep up or things are going to get a little rough for you."

"I am doing the best I can, so just shut up and leave me alone!" Bart sneered.

"Luther, could you hook their horses up to yours and maybe help them keep up?" Jace asked.

Luther said, "I would be glad to. If they give me any trouble, maybe we might just have ourselves an accident."

Fred and Hank caught up with Jace and asked him. "Are you the law?"

"No, I was sent by the sheriff of Hays, Kansas,to bring back the two prisoners."

Hank asked, "What's all this trouble that you've been having? The sheriff told us a little about it."

"I'm not sure. Someone has been out to get me, and I don't know why."

"Do you think it has anything to do with these two men we are bringing back?" Hank asked.

"I don't know why anyone would want to stop me from bringing them back. They're just a couple of saddle tramps."

Fred said,"Maybe it's because you are the shooter."

"I don't think so. I haven't been around much for the last couple of years. I can't think of anyone that would like to kill me now," Jace replied "Hank, how good are the two men we brought with us?"

"They are good men and very dependable," Fred answered.

"I guess I'm getting to where I don't trust anyone lately. Every time I turn around, someone is trying to kill me."

"There has to be some reason you have had so many attempts on your life lately," Hank stated.

"I can't think of any reason, but you are right there must be something. I'm not sure what it is. A few years ago I could think of quite a few reasons some men would like to take a shot at me. I think that is too long ago for them to still be after me, and besides I don't know any that would have the kind of money. You know, to hire all the men that have been after me."

"Well, I guess we better keep our eyes open then," Hank replied.

"Hank, you and Fred is not right. I am going ahead and scout the area just to be on the safe side. I will be back sometime in the morning. Just be careful until then," Jace said.

Jace rode on ahead trying to make sure everything was okay and help the bad feeling go away. He rode most of the morning and saw nothing. He was getting hungry, so he stopped and made a small fire and had some coffee and jerky. He spotted some tracks from shod horses and wondered why so many horses were coming from the direction of town. And, no one had noticed them. The prints were fairly fresh and should have been noticed. Maybe they came around town, but why. They were moving more east, so they should not run on to them. They should be in Phoenix in five or six days.

Jace was riding along watching the trail when Jennifer came to his mind. He found himself wanting to see her again and talk to her. He had never met anyone like her before. He liked thinking about her. He was brought back to reality when heard shots. He thought they sounded like they were just over the next hill. He rode hard until he was almost to the top, pulled his horse to an abrupt stop, and got off his horse. He tied him to a bush and walked to the top and crawled the last few feet until he could see what was going on. A wagon with two or three people were exchanging shots with five mounted men. Jace didn't know who to help. It looked like the folks in the wagon were outnumbered, so he decided to help them.

Jace went back, got his horse, and rode to the crest of the hill. He thought about the situation and decided to just ride in and help the men who were defending the wagon. He pulled his six gun and started riding for the wagon. One of the men on horseback saw him and fired. Jace shot him square in the chest. While he was falling, another was lining up to shoot him. Jace took a quick shot at him. He must have hit him, but not hard enough to bring him down. Jace lay as close to his horse as he could and let him run. When he reached the wagon, Jace jumped off just as a bullet creased his shoulder. He pulled his rifle and headed toward the wagon. There were two men on the ground and one in the wagon. He fell behind a wheel and started shooting when he saw two men fall and hit the ground. A man on horseback picked up one of the men, and they rode away.

An older man by the wagon said, "Thanks, stranger. We were in a bit of trouble 'til you came along. My name is Jake Baker. This is my son Ricky and in the wagon is my daughter Terry."

Jace had not even noticed it was a girl until the old man said his daughter.

"What's the problem, and why were the men after you?" Jace asked.

"Me and my family were headed home when the men jumped us," the old man replied.

"My name is Jace McCord. Why would those men want to harm you and your family?"

Jake said, "We have a little place just a few miles from here and were headed home. The men that jumped us want us off our place so they could have the water and land. We have been there for a long time, even before the Anderson brothers came along. We don't feel like moving on. So me and my family will fight back if necessary," Jake explained.

"I traveling with a group of men, and I was scouting ahead. I need to get back to my men and tell them what I am up to. Maybe we could help you out."

Jake inquired, " Where are you headed?"

"Our next stop is Phoenix," Jace said.

"Our place is on the way, and I could have Ricky go lead your bunch to our place. Terry is a good cook and maybe you all could stay around for a day or two. I don't think the Anderson boys would be to anxious to tackle men that know how to use a gun the way you used yours today."

Jace pondered the situation for a while and finally told the man and his kids that they were taking two men to Kansas for murder. However, he stressed the prisoners were well guarded. "We can't stay too long because I need to get these men to Hays as quick as I can. However, I don't want to see you and your family pushed around by a bunch of no goods like that."

Jake said, "Just tell Ricky where to find your men, and he will bring 'em to our place."

Jace instructed Ricky to tell Fred Barlow what had happened and to bring all of them to the Baker place, even the giant.

Rick took off in a hurry. Jace, the old man, and the girl left for their place. It took them about three hours to reach the ranch. Jake was surprised to find such a nice place. He thought they would probably have a pretty rough looking place, but this was very nice. The house sat on a hill with the barn and other out buildings. At the bottom of the hill was a large lake, which might account for all the trouble with the neighbors. Water was a precious commodity in these parts. They decided it would be late before the rest of them got there.

The horses were put up, and Jace rubbed them down and fed them hay and grain from the barn. While he was rubbing his horse, he thought what a good horse she had been and that maybe he should keep her. When they reached the train, he had planned to sell her and get another when they reached Hays. But to find another horse as good as this one would be difficult. Keeping her would be best, and Jace guessed he would have to name her after all.

Terry came out while Jace was taking care of the horses. She asked," Where are you from?"

"I've traveled around a lot, but I have a place in northern New Mexico."

She asked, "Why have you not been home for so long and are you married?"

"It's a long story; maybe someday I can tell you all about it."

"I would love to hear it. I think I better fix something to eat before your friends get here. I think they will be hungry."

It was late when Hank, Bart, and the rest of the boys rode in. Hank said, "Jace, what seems to be the trouble? Rick said you were jumped by a bunch of gun hands."

"No, I was scouting ahead when I ran across these folks being shot at by a rough bunch. I couldn't just leave them. You boys just stay out of it, and I will see if I can help these folks."

Hank said, "Just try to keep me out of this if you are going to help."

All the rest agreed with Hank. Jake came out and said, "Terry has food on the table if you boys are hungry."

Luther headed toward the house announcing, "I am ready to eat a horse if I had to."

"It would probably be a good idea to feed him before he gets dangerous," Hank laughed, along with the others.

When the men got in the house, there was a big long table to seat several men. Jake said, "This was fixed for the ranch back when we had cowhands working for us."

"I haven't seen anything like this in a long time," Bart said. After they ate, they went to the bunkhouse to get ready for the night.

"It would probably be a good idea if we posted a guard tonight," Jace stated.

"I'll take the first watch," offered Bart.

Hank said he would take the second; then Luther put in for the second shift. That left Jace to take the last watch.

"I have a cellar. We could lock the prisoners in for the night," Jake told them

"That would be a good idea,"Jace replied wearily.

When Luther woke Jace for his watch, he reported seeing four or five men on horses a couple of hours ago but nothing since. Jace said, "I'll keep a good watch just in case."

The next morning they were getting ready for breakfast when Ricky came in and said, "Jace, Tom Anderson and his brothers have a couple of hands with them and are coming down the lane to the house."

Jace went to the porch and leaned on the rail waiting for them to make the first move. Tom Anderson rode up and shouted in a loud voice, "I want to see Jake!"

"I'm talking for him. What seems to be your problem?" Jace replied as he straightened up.

Tom said, "Look, mister, I don't know who you are, but you must be new around here or you'd know not to get smart with me."

"I don't know who you are, and I don't care. Just state your business and get off Jake's property," Jace told him as he let his hand go to the butt of his Colt 45.

'Tom said, "Look mister, you better shut that smart mouth or I'lldo it for you."

"Anytime you think you are man enough."

Tom went for his six-gun, but before he cleared leather he was looking down the barrel of Jace's 45 Colt.

"Hold on, mister. Don't shoot. I never saw anyone that fast before. What's your name?"

"My name is Jason McCord."

"Are you the one they call the Shooter?"

"I've been called that."

Tom said, "Look all I want to do is make Jake an offer on his place."

Jace called Jake out and said, "This feller wants to have a word with you."

"Already told you I don't want to sell, and you aren't offering half what my place is worth anyway."

Tom yelled, "Look, old man, I offered you a fair price and you better take it or else!"

"You better leave and take the trash you brought with you," was Jace's reply.

Tom said, "Look, mister, I don't care who you are and how fast you are with a gun, I want this place and you or nobody else is going to stop me from getting it."

"Any time you're ready and think you're big enough to take it, I'll be ready to let you know you don't always get what you want," Jace replied.

Tom just grunted, motioned for his men, and rode away.

"Jace be careful. He's a very dangerous man, and no tellin' what he might do," Jake warned.

"Are you sure you want to start this, Jake? Once we start there will be no turning back," Jace told him.

"It started a long time ago. Now's a good a time as any to put a stop to it," Jake said as he looked at the men riding away.

Jace asked, "Jim, why don't you go out by the barn and keep

watch." He started to ask the question again and noticed he didn't have Jim's attention. But Terry Baker did. "Jim, I hate to bother you, but we need someone to watch the road." Jim said, "Oh, I'm sorry I will get right on it."

"Honey, you better let that boy keep his mind on his work," Jake replied, and they all laughed.

Terry turned red and said, "I ain't bothering him."

Her brother Ricky smiled. "I think his mind is not on his work. I think you're the one that is bothering him." They all had a good laugh.

Jace said, "Jake, give me the layout of your place and the Anderson brothers. We need to lay out a plan in case they attack us." It took most of the day to get things worked out, but Jace was feeling like a plan was coming together.

"Luther, how are the two prisoners doing?" Jace ask

"They probably need to get out and stretch for a little bit," he answered

"Hank and Les, help give the prisoners a little walk around, feed them, and then throw them back in the cellar."

Luther smiled, "If they give us any trouble, they might get more exercise than they wanted."

Apparently, the prisoners didn't want to tangle with Luther. They followed his orders without a hitch and crawled back into the cellar.

Everything was quiet the rest of the day. That evening they posted watches for the night.

"Could I have a later watch?" I have something to do," Jim asked.

"That'll be fine, but you better be sure what you want before you get to close to that little girl," Jace smiled.

Jim smiled and said, "I really like her. I plan to come back here when we get the men to the train in Santa Fe."

"If that's what you really want to do, that would be fine with me. I met someone in Hays that I really like. But, I know I'm not good for her. She is so beautiful and such a lady that she needs a man that has something to offer her besides being a gunfighter."

Jim questioned, "How do you know if it's the right one?"

"I don't know for sure. It just seems like you want to always be with them and are happier when you are together."

"I feel that way about Terry. I'm going to miss her when we leave. But I will come back to be with her as soon as I can."

"Well,sounds like you may have the right girl then. Just be careful and don't hurt her. You better get some sleep now for your watch."

"Thanks, Jace."

Instead, Jim headed for the house where Terry was. His heart was beating so fast he thought he would pass out when she opened the door as he approached. "Want to take a walk?"

"Sure, but I have to finish supper first."

"Can I help you?"

She said, "That would be very nice."

After they all finished eating and the dishes were washed, Jim took Terry outside. "Terry, I really like you. I know I am just a cowhand and have no right to ask you, but I would like to call on you when we finish this job."

Terry was quiet for a while and then answered him thoughtfully, "I have never felt like I do toward anybody else. I like you a lot, but I can't leave my family. If they get this problem with the Anderson brothers taken care of, they'll be a lot of work to do here. I just can't leave. Jim, you are the most wonderful man I ever met. I would be very happy if you called on me when you can. But you have to understand about my staying here."

"As long as you are here, I could be very happy here or any place you are," Jim replied.

They gazed into each other's eyes for a little while,and then Jim took her in his arms and kissed her tenderly.

Looking into his eyes, Terry said, "I have never felt anything like that before. I know we haven't known each other very long, but I know I already love you."

"Terry, I have never known anyone like you. I have never felt like this before. I feel like my heart is going to jump right out of my body."

She said, "Just hold me for a while. I feel so happy in you're arms, and I don't want to leave right now."

Tom Anderson called his brothers and sneered, "They ain't nobody gonna run me out of this place. I don't care who he is or how bad a gun hand he is. We are gonna take that place away from Jake Baker and his bunch. I think early in the morning we're gonna ride over there and show them smart asses who we are. We'll have that spread when we leave. We can go early and catch them off guard. We are gonna take him before he knows what hit him. Get to bed because we are gonna get an early start."

Jerry worriedly said, "That's Jace McCord, and he's meaner than a box of rattlesnakes and twice as fast."

"He may be fast, but there's a bunch of us and only one of him. The rest of that bunch ain't no worry."

Back at the Baker ranch, Jace was troubled and knew the Anderson boys did't act like to give up a fight easily. "Fred, Hank, come here just a minute. I want to talk to you. We better be ready because the Anderson didn't act like the type to just sit around and take what we dished out to them this afternoon. Go tell the rest of the boys to get ready for an early start in the morning. We will be ready just in case they try anything."

Jace questioned Jake about the direction the Anderson bunch would might come at them from. Jake told him they would probably come at them from the south. That would be the best way in and a good escape in case things didn't work out as they planned.

Jace asked, "What about the west? That's the direction they should come from."

"No, that is some rough country, and I don't think they would try that. Besides if things don't go the way they planed, they wouldn't have a good way to escape. No,I think they would comefrom the south," Jake replied.

Jace said, "I was just checking. I think that's just what they would try, too. We wouldn't be looking for them in that direction. We will set up for that and will leave a couple of men on the south and east. I feel like Tom Anderson is the kind of man that would do just the opposite of what we expected."

Jace walked out to Jim and Terry, filled them in on the plan, and urged them to get to sleep early.

Terry told him, "I'll have breakfast ready when you're ready in the morning."

"Thanks, Terry, see you then," Jace replied as he walked off.

Jim took Terry in his arms and said, "I want you in the house in the morning if they come. I could not stand it if anything happened to you."

She looked in his eyes and said, "How do you think I would feel if anything happened to you? I will always be by my man's side."

He thought aloud, "I like the sound of that…my man."

Terry held him close for a little while and said, "We better take Jace's advice and get some sleep." She paused and asked, "How long have you known Jace?"

Jim said, "I only met him a few days ago in Yuma, but I feel like I have known him a long time."

"I feel the same way. He seems like such a good man and to take the time to help us when he has those two to deliver to jail. Well,good night. I will see you early."

He kissed her, and they left for their beds.

Everyone stood their watch that night. Terry, true to her word, was up early and had breakfast ready for everyone.

Jace told Les and Jim to watch the south just in case, but he felt like the Andersons would come in from the west, the least likely place to come at them.

Jace took Fred and some dynamite that Jake had in his storage shed. They went a ways out and set the charges, so they would have a good advantage on the Anderson boys when they attacked. Jace then positioned everyone else in good places. Jace and his men would be ready for the Anderson bunch.

Tom Anderson gathered his brothers and his men early that morning. "We're going around by Richard's pass and come in that way. Jerry his brother said, "Why are we going that way? It would be a lot easier to come in by the flats."

"That's what they would be expecting. We'll catch 'em by surprise. Besides, I'm in charge here. If that smart mouth McCord says one more word to me, I'll teach him who's boss, too."

Jerry replied, "I don't trust that Jace McCord; he's pretty tricky. He might just pull something."

"Shut up and do what I tell you before I slap the daylights out of you. And that goes for the rest of you, too. We're gettin' real close, and I don't want to spoil our surprise. Slow down now, and we'll go the rest of the way on foot."

Jerry said, "Why don't we just ride in hard and let them have it?"

Tom shook his head, "If you don't shut up, I am going to shoot you first. Why do I have to be kin to so many idiots? Now shut up and be quiet."

Tom yelled, "Look out! They spotted us! Stay low and sneak in on them."

Jace told everyone to be very quiet and wait for the Anderson's to attack. He was getting sleepy waiting,but he could not get up and walk around. Instead, he stretched and tried to think of something to keep him awake. The first thing to come to his mind was Jennifer. And that was a very pleasant thought.

Suddenly, Jace thought he heard a horse shoe click off a rock. He brought all his attention to listening and heard something. hee wasn't sure what it was, but he was ready. After a little while, he could see something move out in the darkness. Now he was sure he saw something. He had to be sure because he would give away their positions as soon as he fired. Yes,now he was sure there was someone out there. He lined his Winchester up and held his breath, afraid to move lest he might miss the first shot. Now he squeezed the trigger; the man went down and did not move.

The Anderson bunch was walking toward the Baker place when the shot was fired. One of Tom's men went down, a gaping hole in his chest.

Then the sky exploded with gun fire, and Jace waited while everyone around him was firing. He placed the charges they had set in his mind. When they were in the right place, he would take them out. Now he held his breath and squeezed the trigger and the charge went off, sounding like the end of the world in the early morning. Jace heard men scream and guns firing. The Anderson bunch started running and were going just as he hoped they would. They were headed towards another charge. Jace sighted on it and let go with another charge. They must have become confused because they were running right in to their line of fire. He heard men scream and go down, bringing back bad memories of the war. After things settled down, Jace called to Tom Anderson and said, "Give up! You're beaten."

Larry Anderson called back and said, "You have killed Tom and Jerry and most of our men. Now, I'm gonna kill you, Jace McCord. In a mad rage, Larry Anderson charged toward Jace, shooting as he came. Jace stood up, pulled his six guns, and shot Larry in the chest. He went down saying, "I'm gonna kill all you that killed my family." Then he fell and didn't move any more."

Everyone just stood there and couldn't speak.

Jace said, "Let's go to the house and rest awhile and then we can bury these men."

Ricky Baker wiped his face, "I never saw anything like that before. I think I am going to be sick."

They rested for a while and then went about their business of burying the men. Les was hit in the arm, and Jake had a flesh wound in the calf of his leg but they weren't serious.

When everything had been tended to, Jace told everyone that they would leave the next morning. He told Hank and Les to take the prisoners out for a walk and feed them and then they would be good until they were ready to leave in the morning.

But the prisoners had some plans of their on. Bart said, "Hank, when they come to take us out for a walk again, we'll jump 'em. If that big monster is not with 'em,we'll make a break for the horses.

"Listen. Someone is coming for us now. We'll take care of that Jace McCord," Hank replied with hate in his voice.

Bart said, "They ain't done such a good job so far. I think we can take them if they're not with that big feller."

"Okay, we we'll give it a try. Sounds like the battle is over. I can hear them talking so I don't guess they killed any of 'em."

Bart said hopefully, "Maybe they killed that big man, or Jace. Maybe we finally got lucky."

"Well, we''l see soon."

Hank and Les opened the door to the cellar and told the two prisoners to come on up. Nothing happened, so they both hollered again. No answer.

Hank said, "You don't think they escaped, do you? We were mighty busy this morning,and they might have found a way out of here."

Les shook his head, "I don't know, but looks like we're gonna have to find out." He walked down the stairs with Hank right behind him. They couldn't see anything in the dark. But suddenly, Les felt like the house fell on him. Hank had both prisoners on him before he could think. Overpowering Les and Hank, he two ran up the stairs and headed toward the barn and the horses Just as they rounded the corner of the barn, the prisoners ran smack into Luther. He picked them up by their shirts and banged their heads together. The two went down like they had been shot. Luther drug them back to the house and called for Jace.

Jace came running, noticed the two prisoners on the ground and asked, "What's goin' on, Luther?"

Luther answered, "I think they was trying to get away, but they found me first. I think we need to check on Hank and Les."

Just about that time, Les came up the stairs carrying Hank. He said, "They jumped us and took off."

Jace asked, "Why didn't you call for help before you got in trouble?"

Les said "I see now that's what we should have done. Next time I won't take any chances."

"I'll throw them in the cellar, and this time they'll stay there until we get ready to get on our way," Luther said as he gave them a hard look.

Terry Baker came out of the house and announded, "I have supper ready if you are ready to eat."

"I'm always ready to eat," Luther replied as he pushed the two men toward the cellar.

"I don't think we have enough to fill him up," Jace laughed as they all headed towards the house.

Jake ask Jace, "When do you plan on leaving?"

He replied, "Probably early in the morning."

They had a lot of things to get ready, but Jace thought they could be ready by morning. He asked Jake if he wanted to file a claim on the Anderson Brothers land. While Jake didn't know if he could do that, he was certainly interested in having more land.

Jace said, "Why don't you let Rick go with us to Phoenix and file claim on the land? I'll fill out work about what happened, and you shouldn't have any trouble getting title to the land."

"I'd like that," chimed in Rick. " And, I think I will have some company on the way back anyhow," laughed Rick.

Everyone looked at Jim and laughed as he turned red and said, "It's no secret that I care for Terry very much." She took her turn to turn red. Everyone had a good laugh and finished supper.

"We need to get ready to leave early,so we better get a good night sleep," Jace announced.

Rick said, "I'll be ready anytime you're ready to leave in the morning."

Jim called Terry outside and said, "I'd like to talk to you for a minute." When she came out, he took her in his arms and kissed her.

Finally putting away from his kiss, Terry said, "I'm going to miss you, Jim. I want you to promise me that you'll be very careful and come back to me."

Jim smiled, "Do you really want me to come back with your brother?"

She held him and kissed him again and said, "I want that more than anything else."

He was just about ready to kiss her when her father Jake came around the corner. Jim tried to say something, but nothing came out. Jake laughed to himself and told Terry to go see if she could help the men get ready to leave in the morning.

Jim started to leave, too, but Jake said, "Hold on. I want to talk to you. I think I know how you feel about my daughter. I'm happy about that because you seem like a good boy. What I wanted to know, if I get that land of the Anderson's,I'm goin' to need more help. If you and Terry are planning on being together, then we can have a good place. You, me and Rick can handle most of the work,but we will still need some extra hands."

"Mr. Baker, I know I love your daughter more than I ever cared about anyone in my life. If she will have me, I plan on asking her to marry me when I get back," Rick answered.

"Well, I don't think you will have a problem in getting' the answer you want. I never seen her act like that toward anyone else. She likes Jace and the rest of the boys, but she don't treat them like she does you. I will be glad when you and Rick get back safe, so we can get started on our ranch. Oh, and, I'd be glad to have you in the family, too."

After they had finished their supper and everything was taken care of,Jace told Ricky he wanted to talk before they left in the morning. He said, "Before you start out with us in the morning,I want to warn you that I have been attacked ever since I left Hays. I don't know why. It may be someone that has an old grudge from the past. I just can't figure out who because it would take a lot on money and a lot of hate to keep after me all this way. We may be hit again before we get to Phoenix. I just wanted you to know about it before hand."

Rick said, "Don't worry about me.I can take care of myself and maybe an extra gun might come in handy. Besides, I have a new brother- in- law to look out after."

Jace laughed, "I think you may be right. I think you're getting a good one." They talked a while and Jace said they had better get some sleep to be fresh for an early start next morning.

Terry took Jim out to the barn and told him, "I have a bad feeling about you and the rest of these men leaving in the morning and I don't want to loose you."

He kissed her and smiled, "I will be back as soon as they catch the train in Santa Fe. I have never found anyone like you, and I am not about to loose you now." He kissed her again and held her in his arms and told her everything wouldbe all right. "I have never seen anyone like Jace and he will take care of every thing. He is a very dangerous man to make an enemy of. If anyone jumps us they will be very sorry." He started to pull back and look into her eyes, but she would not let go. Jim just held her close. He told her how much he loved her.

She looked at him and said, "That's the first time you told me you loved me. I love you so very much, and I want to always have you by my side. Dad and Rick like you, too. I haven't found very many men that my dad approved of when it came to me. That's a good sign, don't you think?"

He said, "I guess so, and I like them too. Besides, I've always wanted a brother. Maybe Rick can my brother?"

Luther went to the basement to check on the prisoners. When he opened the door, they were ready to jump him until they saw who it was. Then, they backed off and sat down. He told them to come on and get some exercise. Luther would have enjoyed a good fight, but they didn't act like they were interested. He told them if they were good little boys, he would bring them something to eat; but if they weren't good, he would wait until morning before he fed them.

Hank said, "We'll be good because I am hungry and could eat the south end of a north bound mule."

"I'll be back in a little while with your food, and I'll be bringing it. If you want to jump me when I get back, go for it. We will have some fun, and you will loose your supper or eat it off the floor when I spill it," Luther laughed.

Jace woke and thought it must be around five o'clock. He started getting his things together.

Jim and Les woke up and ask. "What time is it?"

"I think it must be about five," Jace told them. "Go ahead and get your things ready, and I'll see about getting us something to eat." He walked to the well, washed his face, and heard someone behind him. He had his hand on the butt of his Colt when he heard Terry say, "It's just me. I am fixing you all a good breakfast and need some water for coffee."

"That sounds real good. Thanks," Jace replied.

Terry smiled and pleaded, "Jace, please take good care of Jim and send him back to me safe. I care for him very much."

He laughed and told her, " Don't worry. I'll take good care of all them. I already figured out that you care about each other."

She hugged Jace and said, "Thank you for all you have done for us. Now we can live a good life without someone trying to take it all away from us."

"That's okay. I don't like bullies and men that think they can push people around any way they want to. I can tell you this: Jim is a mighty lucky fellow to have such a wonderful girl in love with him. I wish you both all the happiness in the world."

Terry asked, "Jace, do you have anyone in your life?"

"I met someone in Dodge before I left to get these prisoners. I don't know how she feels about me, but I like her a lot. I don't think it will work out because she is such a wonderful girl, and

I am just a drifter and gun hand. That's not the kind of life I want, but it seems like it follows me wherever I go."

She said, "Just from what I can see of you and your life, I think she cares for you unless she just doesn't know what a good thing is. As for you being a drifter and gun hand, I think you are a very wonderful man who helps other people wherever you are."

He gave her a hug and said, "Thanks, I better make sure everyone is getting ready."

"I'll have breakfast ready very soon," she said.

Jace told Luther to get the prisoners ready. After they ate, they would be on their way.

Luther opened the door to the basement and said, "You two come on up here; we are getting ready to leave. So let's go. Now! If you want something to eat before we go."

They came up the stairs, complaining about getting up so early. Luther grabbed them by the shirt collars and gave them a shove towards the well, telling them to get washed up and ready for the last good meal any of them were likely to have for a while.

Terry had breakfast ready and set out on some tables and chairs they used out side.

Luther said, "Boy, look at that breakfast—eggs and bacon and gravy and good hot coffee and real biscuits. I ain't had nothing like that in a real long time. Miss Terry, we sure do thank you for such good meals that you have been fixin' for us while we've been here."

Terry went to Luther and gave him a big hug. "Luther, we are the ones that should be thankful for all you and your friends have done for us while you were here. We'll miss all of you very much. Jace asked, "Why don't you and your family come to see us sometime? We would like that very much."

After they finished eating, they loaded the horses and were ready to leave. Jake said, "You boys are welcome here anytime, and we might come to see you someday if we get a time when we are caught up. Well, so long for now and hope to see you all sometime down the road. You keep a sharp look out on your back trail now. Jim, we will see you soon as you finish your job with Jace and get back here."

As they watched them ride away, Terry hugged Jake and told him, "Daddy, I am so worried about them, and I really do care for Jim. I just don't want anything to happen to any of them."

He said, "Honey I think they will be alright. That Jace is a very good man, and I think he can handle any thing that comes their way."

"Do you think Rick will have any trouble getting the title to the Anderson's land?" she asked her father.

He answered, "I don't think so because Jace said he knew a good lawyer in Hays."

"I think that is the father of the girl he likes. If I know anything about women, I think she likes him too," Terry grinned.

"Well, we will know soon how it'll all turn out. I'm going to check around for some good hands just in case we need them," Jake replied.

"Where would be a good place to look for new hands?"

He told her, "I think some of the boys on the Anderson spread might be interested, so I'll go check with them."

"Daddy, be real careful. Some of them might be unhappy about their bosses being killed by you and your family."

"I know of a couple that might, but I think the most of them will be glad to be rid of the brothers because they could be a mean lot. I will be back as soon as I can."

Rick rode up beside Jace and said, "I worry about dad and Terry while I'm gone."

"I think they'll be okay. You said the Anderson brothers were the only bad people that you had to deal with. So unless some one new rides in, I think they will be okay. We'll get you home as soon as we can. I'll telegraph Fred Lawson as soon as we get to Phoenix. I think he can tell us how to take care of everything. We should be there some time next week, and you can be on your way home soon. I hope that in a couple of months Jim can be back with you and your family. I better see how Luther is getting along with the prisoners."

He rode up to him and asked, "You doing okay with these ole' boys?"

"Yeah, they ain't no trouble when you talk to them right."

Jace laughed and said, "I guess you just have a way with words."

Bart growled, "I don't like the way we are being treated."

"If you don't shut up, you are going to like it even less," was Luther's answer.

Lem said, "Did you see where they went?"

"Yes," Harry replied. "They left that bunch of farmers this morning, and they should be here early in the morning.We had better get ready. They picked up another rider with them."

"Who is it?" Lem asked.

"I don't know, but you should have seen the way they took care of the old boys that attacked them a couple of mornings ago. They ain't going to be easy to take care of."

"Just shut up and leave the thinking to me. That's what I'm being paid for. We'll wait for them on that hill behind those rocks. That will be as good a place as any to ambush them," Lem told them.

Jim rode up beside Rick and said, "I hope your dad and Terry will be okay 'til you get back home."

"Yeah, I do to. Jace told me he thought they would be fine

'til I can get back. You really do like my sister, don't you?" Rick questioned.

"Yes,I do. I think she is the most wonderful girl I ever met, and I hope to spend my life with her."

Rick said, "I hope so. Too. Dad really likes you, and I do, too. With you in the family, we could have a good chance at a really good ranch and be able to do some of the things we always wanted to do."

"You know, Rick, it sounds almost too good to be true. I have always wanted a home and a family. My family was killed a few years ago in an Indian raid. I would really like to be part of your family."

"Well,if my sister has any thing to do about it,I think you will be," Rick laughed.

Jace said, "I am going to scout ahead . You all keep your eyes open because I don't like the feeling I have."

Rick asked, "Do you know something we don't?"

"No, it's just a feeling I got when I was in the war. Just like I felt when we were walking into an ambush."

"I have heard about how some of you could feel trouble before it came."

"Well, just pass the word that I will be back soon, and you all need to keep your eyes open." He rode on ahead and looked around but didn't find anything that looked out of place. Still, he couldn't shake that feeling. He rode over a little rise and spotted a creek and a few trees and thought that wouldl be a good place to stop for dinner and rest for a while. He rode back and told the rest of them that he found a good place to stop and eat.

They stopped and unsaddled their horses.

Jace said, "I think it would okay to build a fire and have a hot meal and coffee."

While they were eating, Hank came over and sat down by Jace and inquired, "You know Rick said you had a bad feeling about something but couldn't put your finger on it. Well, I've had a bad feeling in the back of my neck, too. Do you think we are headed into trouble?"

"I don't know," Jace answered him. "Hank it's just a feeling I get sometimes. You were in the war too, weren'tyou?"

"Yeah, I was and that is where I started getting these feelings about danger. I can't explain it, but it is just a feeling that something is not right."

Jace replied, "I know the feeling. I can't tell you why I feel that way, but it's like something is wrong, and I have no reason to think that. Just keep everyone alert for danger just in case."

They finished eating and saddled the horses that had been grazing on some grass down by the creek. Then, they headed out. Jace rode beside Luther and said, "Why don't you keep the prisoners back a ways just in case we run into trouble. That way you can get them and yourself under cover."

"If there is any trouble,I want to help," Luther said.

"I want to keep those two safe, so they can go to trial and hang for the murder in Hays."

"Okay," Luther answered. "I'll see they are safe. Do you think we will run into trouble?"

"I don't know; it's just a feeling I have, so be careful."

Jace told everyone, "I am going on ahead and check things out, so keep a look out."

He rode on ahead and scouted around. He was not sure what was causing the feeling he had, but it was something he had learned to pay attention to in the past. He found that most of the time when the feeling was this strong, it usually meant something.

Jace found some pretty country, but no trouble that he could see. Still there was some thing bothering him, and he was going to find what ever it was. It was very hot and the sun blazing down was almost more than a body could take at times. He was almost out of water, but they needed a place to camp for the night so he would look a little farther. He was climbing a pretty good hill decided to see what was on the other side before turnong back. Just as he topped the hill, Jace thought he spotted a horse and rider; however, the sun was so bright maybe it was just a reflection or something. He saw some trees in a row and thought maybe there might be some water near. He rode down to check and found asmall stream,which might be the same one they stopped at to eat earlier. Suddenly, he spotted some fresh tracks. Jace got down from his horse to take a closer look. They were tracks of a man and a shoed horse, so it was not an Indian. But, that didn't take away the bad feeling he still had.

Jace saw his bunch coming over a rise and thought he would just wait for them.

When they got to him he said, "Just ahead a ways is a good place to make camp for the night. I spotted some tracks of a horse and rider. The horse had shoes and the man wore boots, so it's not an Indian. I can't find anything else but keep your eyes open just in case."

They started toward the place Jace told them about and Bart said, "I am hot and need to rest."

"If you don't shut up, it is going to get a lot hotter for you," Luther smiled.

Hank yelled, "You can't talk to us that way!"

Luther reached over,slapped him, and said, "Who's going to stop me? I've had just about all I am going to take from you, so you just keep your mouth shut and we will get along just fine."

They made camp and while the others started cooking, Jace and Les took care of the horses and hobbled them in a meadow that was close by. They would be fine since away from the stream there was nothing but desert. They finished eating, and Jace was having another cup of coffee and talking about the rest of the trip.

Jace stated, "I just can't shake this bad feeling, so we need to post a watch tonight and keep a close watch during the day."

Hank asked,"Do you think maybe I better scout on ahead tomorrow and keep a look out for trouble?"

"No, I think we need to stay together in case we run into trouble. I don't want to get separated in case of trouble. We better get some sleep because we have a big day ahead of us tomorrow."

"How are we going to keep an eye on our prisoners tonight?" Luther asked.

"Whoever is on watch can keep an eye on them. Plus, we'll tie 'em together. Then to one of us just in case they try to escape. Even if they did get away, they couldn't get to the horses before the person on watch heard them and stopped them. And, without horses, they couldn't get very far. If they do get very far, the person on watch can just shoot them." Jace thought that might keep them close.

Luther tied the two men together and then around his leg and said, "Good night, boys. Sleep good, but don't have too much moving around. If you wake me, I'll get very unhappy."

Jace had the last watch and just before dawn he built a fire and started some hot water for coffee. When the coffee started brewing, he heard some of the crew moving around. They were all ready by daylight and started to move again. They came over a rise and Jace stopped and frowned. "I don't like the road ahead. There is a big rise ahead with a lot of cover,and the road to that hill is open with no cover."

Hank rode up to Jace and said, "I have a feeling in the back of my neck like when were riding into an ambush in the war."

"I know what you mean because I have the same feeling."

"What do you think we should do, Jace?"

"Let's move to the right a ways because there are some rocks we could use for cover if we have to."

They started out, and Jace moved back to Luther and told him, "Hold back with the prisoners just in case we are jumped ahead."

Luther asked, "You expecting trouble?"

"I don't know,but Hank and I have a bad feeling about the road ahead, and we are going to move to the right just in case. I noticed the ground ahead is pretty open and a good place for an ambush."

In the rocks ahead, Lem told Harry to get ready because they were coming. Harry said, "Look,they are going off the road. do you think they spotted us?"

"I don't think so. I think that feller leading them is smarter than I gave him credit for, but we can still make this work. Just take more time and aim for longer range shots."

Harry said, "I'll tell the rest of the boys, and we will get them all before we stop."

"Be sure not to hit them two fellers we was sent to get," Lem replied.

"Okay," Harry said. "Let's just get ready."

Jace was very jumpy for some reason. Just keep calm he kept telling himself. Maybe you are just too overly careful. They had gone about two hundred yards when gun fire broke out. He saw Jim Taylor hit the ground, but he didn't have time to see how bad he was hit. Jace fell behind a boulder and tried to see where the shots were coming from.

Terry yelled, "Jace, Jim's been hit! I don't think it's too bad, but I can't get the bleeding stopped."

"Wrap it tight and hold pressure on it to stop the blood." Hank answered.

"You all keep your heads down, and I am going to try to make my way around behind them and see if I can find out what 's going on, and who is shooting at us." Jace crawled behind rocks until he came to a place that was open for about 150 feet. He got on his feet and bunched his muscles for a fast get away to make it to the next rocks. He jumped and ran as hard as he could. Bullets were flying all around him. He felt a sting in his right calf, but he didn't think it was very bad. He ran behind what rocks he could find and made his way up the hill around whoever was doing the shooting. He could hear fire coming from his group, and he was worried about them. But, he had to think about what he was doing. He heard shooting just up and around from where he was. He ran up to a large rock and eased around the side where he could look down on whoever was shooting at them. Jace could see five men, but he heard shooting to the left, too. There was at least one more. He contemplated the situation; he couldn't just shoot them in the back. He took his rifle and eased to a tree and yelled, "I have you covered. Throw down your guns!"

The five men he could see were surprised and could not move for a minute. But, a large man with a rough face and shoulders like a bull brought his rifle up to shoot. Jace shot him in the chest and watched him slam back against the rock. Hedidn't move ever again. The man on the end away from Jace drew his six gun and tried to fire, but Jace caught him between the eyes. Then, he shot one of the others that tried to get a shot at him. The other two raised their hands and yelled, "Don't shoot mister!"

Jace moved out from behind the tree and watched the two men with their hands up. He said, "Drop your guns." They dropped the rifles, and he told them, "Now your six guns." They didn't make a move to drop their guns from their holsters. Jace thought something was wrong, but by he could assess the situation, something caught his eye. The man behind the rock had him dead in his sight. He didn't have time to swing around and shoot before the man could shoot him.

Jace was ready for the shot to end his life when he heard a shot more to the left and saw the man go down. He was stunned, and he saw the two men he was holding a gun on go for their guns. He shot twice, and both men went down. One of the men said, "Help me! I'm gut shot." Jace heard something behind him and drew his six gun and fell to the ground. He slid sideways to fire when Fred Barlow yelled out, "Don't shoot! It's me."

Jace got to his feet and asked, "Was that you that shot the man behind that rock?"

"Yeah, I had to. He was going to shoot you."

"You saved my life."

"Yeah, I know now I own you by some of the customs of those foreign countries," and he laughed.

"Thanks, maybe I can repay you sometime." Jace went to the man on the ground that had been gut shot and asked, "Why were you trying to kill us?"

"Please help me! I'm hurtin' worse than I can stand."

Fred told him, "Let me look at that wound, I patched up a lot of our boys in the war."

"Please help me! I hurt so bad and don't want to die."

Fred said, "Here, I am going to help you, so you help us. Who sent you to kill us?"

"I don't know. But the man behind the rock that you shot was the one that was in charge," he told them.

He didn't know any more except they were to be careful and not hit the prisoners.

"I am going to check on the rest of our bunch. Will you be okay?" Jace asked.

"Yeah," Fred replied ."But this looks bad. I don't know how much I can help him."

Jace came down the rocks and yelled at his bunch down the hill and asked, "Are you all alright?"

Ricky said, "Come on down; we have problems."

Jace ran down to them and found Les Johnson laying on the ground with blood running out of his mouth. He said something that Jace could not hear, so he got down with his ear next to his mouth. Les said, "Would you tell my brother in Yuma that I love him and am sorry for any thing that I've done wrong."

"Yes, but you can tell him yourself. Someone go get Fred and tell him to come help Les."

Ricky took off up the hill to get Fred and bring him back. Les started coughing and was gone. Everyone was in shock and Jace told everyone, "We'll bury him here and notify his brother where to find him."

"Jace, come here Jim has been hit. He's not too bad, but he lost quite a bit of blood and is very weak." Luther said as he put more bandages on Jim's wound.

Jace knelt down and said, "How you doing Jim?"

"Just a little blood gone. But I'll be alright."

"You better be or there is a little girl back up the trail that would never forgive me if you weren't," Jace laughed.

Jim smiled, "I hope she will be waiting for me when I get back after we get the prisoners to Phoenix."

"This is as far as you are going. I am sending you, and Ricky home with someone to help you."

Ricky walked up and said, "I think you'll need all the help you can get, so we better stay with you."

"No, you take Jim home with you. I think he needs some rest and tender loving care. Do you know someone that would be willing to take care of that?"

Ricky laughed, "I think I can find someone that could fill the bill." They all laughed.

Fred said, "I think he will be just fine."

"I will send Hank with you to help you get home."

Ricky said, "No, I think Jim and I will be just fine. I know this country real good, and I can take him home with no trouble. I think you are going to need all the help you can get to take these two skunks back to Hays."

"Well, we'll stay here tonight and all get an early start in the morning."

They made camp. Taking his gun, Ricky announced, "I'll go find some game for supper." And, he left.

"I don't think you will have any trouble but be careful. Let's bury Les and find something to mark his grave, so his brother can find him," Jace remarked as he stood up.

Fred made a fire and put on some coffee. They waited for Ricky to get back with some fresh meat for supper. They were sitting around talking when suddenly Jace said, "Quiet, I hear something just over the hill."

He went up the hill almost to the top and lay on his stomach and crawled to the top where he could look over and see what was making the noise. He eased his rifle over and sighted in on the noise as Ricky said, "Don't shoot! It's me, Ricky."

Jace stood up and saw Ricky had a nice buck over his shoulders. He ran to help him take it back to camp. Everyone had a good meal and got ready to sleep.

Fred said, "Do you think we should put out a watch tonight?"

"I think those that we shot today were all, and I think we will be safe for tonight anyhow."

"Why are they trying to get us and take the prisoners?" Hank asked.

"I don't know unless someone wants them for killing a family member or a friend or something like that. Whatever the reason, we need to be careful the rest of the trip. When we get to Phoenix, I am going to talk to the sheriff and see if he will keep them in his jail for a couple of days and let us rest up for the rest of the trip. We really need to find someone to help us the rest of the way."

Ricky said, "I know a couple of fellers that might help you." He gave Jace the names and said,"Tell them I sent you."

They all had a good night's sleep and were ready to leave just after sunup. Jim and Ricky said their good-byes to everyone and said they would miss them. Jace replied, "Maybe we will see you someday before to long."

Jace and his bunch headed toward Phoenix and hoped they did not run into any more trouble since they were short- handed. Maybe they could get the two men in Phoenix that Ricky told them about.

Fred rode up beside Jace and asked, "Do you think we will have any more trouble?"

"I don't think so, but keep your eyes open just in case. By the way, how is Luther making out with the two prisoners?"

"Don't worry about Luther; he can handle any four men I ever saw." They laughed

Jace said, "Let's keep an eye on them just in case. They are pretty sneaky, and they might try something unexpected."

They made it pretty well for a couple of days; then they ran short on water. Jace said, "I'm going to scout for water so be careful while I am gone."

"How're you going to find water in this desert?" Fred asked.

"I am going to look for game trails that will lead us to some water. It might just be a pool in the rocks or a spring, but animals know where water is. I will try to be back by late tonight if possible. If I am not back by sundown, make camp and head out early in the morning." Jace took all the canteens, except two and headed out. He rode for a couple of hours before he ran on to a trail that looked good enough to follow. Sometimes the trail was so narrow he had to lead his horse through the rocks and brush. Just as he topped a hill, Jace saw what he was searching for, a pool of water. He rode down and let his horse drink first. Then he took off his shirt and gun, lay down, and stuck his head in the water. The water was cool and refreshing, so it must be spring fed. Jace loosened the saddle and let the horse graze in the lush grass around the water. He lay back on the grass, and Jennifer came to his mind. She was a very wonderful girl, and he could not get her off his mind. He would find himself smiling while thinking about her. How could he even think about her? How could he find happiness with the kind of life he lived? He had lost one wife to violence, so what made him think he could ever find happiness again? But he could kee thought of Jennifer from filling his head. He could wish, at least.

Jace's rifle lay beside him in case of trouble, but he was in deep thought when a big buck came to drink. The venision would be a good meal for tonight, along with the cool, fresh water. He eased the rifle up and got the deer in his sights. He squeezed the trigger, the big buck fell, tried to get up, but fell back and did not move again. Just then a big doe walked up, and Jace shot her, too. As he walked to his horse, he felt something wrong. He looked in the brush and spotted four braves watching him. They were Apache, and he knew they could be very dangerous. He held up his hand in a sign of peace. They stood watching him for what seemed like an hour, but he knew it was just a short while. One of the braves held his hand in a sign of peace and made a sign like eating. Jace understood they were hungry. He used sigh language to tell them to come on, and they could share the meat. He cut the buck up and took a hindquarter and told them they could have the hide and the rest of the meat and the doe. That seemed to make them happy. The Indians brought their horses up and loaded the meat and hide. Giving the peace sign again, they rode off. Jace did not understand why they were so hungry with game that plentiful, but there must be a reason. He rode back to catch up with his group and have a good meal and think about what they might find in Phoenix When he rode into camp with the water and deer meat, the men jumped and yelled, "We'll eat good tonight."

Jace said, "Someone might think you boys are hungry."

Luther came over and said, "Here let me help you with the meat."

They all laughed. "I guess it takes more to fill up a big man."

"Now you're learning. I think I could eat that whole hindquarter," Luther laughed, as he lifted the meat to the ground. They all had a good laugh.

Hank said, "I will get the fire started and put some coffee on. Then we can cook the meat and try to fill that human giant up with what ever we can find."

"I think we have some potatoes and beans to go with that," Fred told them.

"Sounds mighty good to me," Jace smiled.

After they finished eating, Jace went to check the horses and get ready for a good night's sleep. After everyone was finished and were all getting ready for bed, Jace told them about the Indians.

Fred replied, "I'll tell you why them Indians are hungry. It's because John Lassiter of the Rocking L is trying to run the Indians out of the area, so he can claim all the land that belongs to them."

"What about the army? Why don't they put a stop to that?" Jace asked.

"They are in Lassiter's pocket. The major in charge is being paid off to force the Indians out of the area."

"Do the Indians not fight back, after all we are talking about apaches," Jace wondered.

"They've tried, but the army chases them down and shoots all they can catch. They can't stop long enough to find food and if Lassiter finds out you helped the Indians, he will be after you."

"Good, let him start something with me. He will wished he had left well enough alone."

"But Jace he has the army backing him and also he has a lot of men working for him. Have you seen the men he has working for him? They're a mean looking bunch," Fred explained.

"But are any of them gunfighters? There is a big difference between cow hands and gunfighters.

"I don't know." Fred replied.

Jace said, "I doubt they are, and they will scare off pretty quick."

"What about the army though?"

"I know a couple of generals. Maybe they can help us," Jace answered

Luther smiled, "I'm ready for a good fight. All this baby sitting is getting on my nerves."

Everyone had a good laugh and got their bedrolls down and were ready for a good night's sleep. It had been a long day, and everyone was very tired. They went to sleep.

Jace woke early and started getting the horses and saddles together for an early start. Luther was up getting the prisoners up and ready. Fred sat up, "I'll get a fire started and get breakfast ready."

By the time the horses were ready, they sat down and ate biscuits, salt pork and coffee.

They rode steady and made good time. At dusk the group made camp that night and had an early start the next morning. About ten Fred told everyone, "I'm going to scout ahead and will be back soon."

"Be very careful," Jace warned.

Just after lunch time, Fred came back and said he came to a town called Palo Verde.

"How big is the town?" Jace asked

"It's not a big town, but it does have a couple stores and two saloons, along with a good café and a dry goods store for supplies."

"Good," Jace replied. "We could use some supplies and maybe a good meal at a café"

"How long before we get to Phoenix?" Hank asked.

"I figure it will take us a couple of days out of Palo Verde to reach Phoenix."

They reached Palo Verde late that evening and found a place they could all stay the night. After they took care of the horses and ate, Jace told them, "Keep a good watch because we don't know anyone here. Someone may try for the prisoners again. I'll be back in a while. I'm going to go check around town and see if I can pick up on any gossip. Sometimes you can pick up some good information around town."

"You care if I go with you?" Hank asked

"No, come along. Be glad for the company."

As they walked, Jace ask Hank, "Would you like a drink? Sometimes the best place to hear gossip is in a saloon."

"Sure, I'd like that."

They found what appeared to be the best place for a drink. When they walked in, Jace moved over to stand with his back to the wall until his eyes adjusted to the dim light inside. They went to the bar and ordered a beer and watched the poker games. It was crowded with several tables of 4, 5, or 6 men playing at each table. One old man came to the bar and ordered a beer and the bar keep said, "Get out, Charlie, you know I can't give you anymore credit."

He begged, "Please, just one for the road."

"No, you already owe the house too much now. Get out before there is trouble."

Jace smiled, "Here old timer. Let me buy you a drink."

"Bless you son. I sure do appreciate it. You all new in town?"

"We just rode in this evening."

"Well, if your stayin' long let me tell you to be careful. There's this ole boy here that scares everyone and he's fast with a gun. Nobody wants to make him mad and that ain't hard to do."

"Thanks for the warning mister. What is this bad man's name just in case we run across him?"

"His name's Jimmy Hanson, but he calls hisself the kid."

"Well thanks,old timer. We will be on the look out for him."

"By the way, what is your name mister?"

"My name is Jace."

"It seems I heard that name before. I can't place where I heard it. It'll come to me."

"Well, thanks again Charlie. Maybe we will see you again before we leave."

They started toward the door and the old man yelled, "Wait, I got it. Jace McCord the shooter!"

The place was suddenly quiet. Jace shook his head. "Oh, no, I was hoping to get out with out being noticed."

"Seems like everybody knows you Jace," Hank replied,

"Well, let's get back to our friends and maybe we can get the supplies we need early and get out before anything else happens."

When they got back to the room where they were staying, everyone eagerly wanted to hear any news they had. "Well, everyone in town knows Jace is here and if there's anyone looking for us, they know we are here," Hank said.

"Just let'em come," Luther laughed. "We'll bang their heads together."

They had a good night's sleep and were up early. Jace took Fred and Hank to the café to have breakfast. He asked, "Luther, if you don't mind, we will have breakfast and then while Fred and Hank gather up supplies for us, I'll come back and help you take the prisoners to eat."

"That's fine, Jace. We will be ready when you come back."

They found a place that looked clean and looked like they had good food. They went in and found a table in the corner, so they would have their backs to the wall.

A girl came over as ask, "Would you like coffee?"

They all said yes.

"Jace, I have this feeling like something is not right. Like maybe something is going to happen."

"I know," Jace replied, "I feel the same way. Let's just eat and get supplies while Luther and the two prisoners eat and then we will get going."

They finished breakfast, and Jace left to get Luther and the prisoners. He walked in and Luther jumped up, "Well we're ready to go. You know me I'm always ready to eat."

Jace laughed, "Keep a sharp eye out; I have a bad feeling."

"Okay, Jace, I'll watch these two and you watch our backs."

"Maybe somebody will shoot you. You big bastard. I am tired of you pushing us around," Bart sneered.

Luther slapped him, "I told you to keep your mouth shut because the next time I will fix you so you can't talk. Now if you want to eat get moving and don't give us any trouble, if not I will put you back in the jail until we get through eating."

"No," Burt said. "I'm hungry."

They went to the café and ordered breakfast. The girl that waited on them ask about the two men and why they looked so rough.

"Well, ma'am they can't keep out of trouble," Luther smiled.

They finished eating. Jace paid for their meals, and they left. They went to the livery and got the horses ready and went to the store to get Hank and Fred. They were just about ready to leave when a voice from the street said, "Well, well, if it ain't the great Jace McCord."

Jace turned and saw this kid standing in the middle of the road with two guns hanging on his hips. He didn't say anything, but he was thinking I don't want to kill this kid. Why can't he just leave us alone.

The kid yelled, "I think your yellow that's what I think!"

Jace just stood there and didn't say anything. Sometimes these kids would just talk themselves out of a gunfight, but it didn't look like this kid was going to give up.

"You heard me McCord. I said you're yellow."

A crowd had gathered by this time and some were thinking this man was dead because when you made the kid mad you better say you were sorry or he'd shoot you. They were all afraid of him. He had run over people in this town until no one would stand up to him. He was faster than anyone, and no one could beat him in a gunfight.

Jace just looked at him and didn't say anything.

It made the kid madder and he was yelling louder, "You're

yellow, and I aim to prove it to everybody in town. The great Jace McCord backed down form the Kid."

Jace was tired of this game and started walking toward him. This made the kid nervous, and he started holding his hands just above the handles of his Colts. He couldn't stand still. Jace knew then he had him. If he was going to make a move, he would have already done it. He kept walking and the kid said, "Stop or I will kill you."

Jace just laughed and said, "You're just a big mouth. If you had any guts you would have pulled them pistols by now. He kept walking. The kid didn't know what to do. Jace walked right up to him and slapped him hard across the face. The kid started to reach for his guns, but Jace slapped him again and took his pistols away from him.

The kid started crying and fell on his knees. He said, "Please don't shoot me I don't want to die."

Jace looked at the people on the street and said, "Is this what you people have been so afraid of? Look at your fears. Most of the time it's things you don't need to fear. Men get to acting tough and people are afraid of them and don't need to be. You have to watch because sometimes a man is really bad, and you should be careful of them, but you don't need to let one or two men push the whole town around. Stand together, and you can keep your self respect."

Jace told the kid, "You better be careful in this town because somebody will kick your ass. They know now you are all mouth. If I was you, I'd be very careful. I don't think this town will cow down to you anymore. If I hear that you have hurt anyone, I will come back and finish what I started. I suggest you be careful and be a good boy. "

They rode out headed for Phoenix. They were ready to get there and have a little rest. They rode for the rest of that day and the next day. Fred told Jace he would scout ahead.

"Be careful," Jace said

Fred was back in about an hour, very excited. He told them, "The town is just over the next rise."

They rode into town,a tired dusty lot. Jace spotted the building that said sheriff's office and told them he was going to call on the sheriff. He walked in and a tall man with wide shoulders and a powerful frame almost ran over him.

"I'm sorry. I'm the sheriff of Phoenix, Justin Barnes."

"Sheriff, do you have a minute? I would like to talk to you, if I could?"

"I was headed over to the café to have lunch. Would you like to join me?"

"I really need to talk before we go."

"Okay," the sheriff replied. "Sit down and tell me what's on your mind."

Jace told him about their prisoners and the trouble they had along the way.

Justin stood and moved toward Jace and stuck out his hand. "I should have known your name, but now I know who you are. You are the one they call Shooter."

"Yeah, I am afraid so."

"Be very careful around here .I hear John Lassiter is looking for you. Something about you helping the Indians," Justin warned.

"I didn't know it was against the law to help them. Besides with them all around me, I felt it was the best thing to do."

"Don't get me wrong, Jace, I'd like to put a stop to Lassiter and his bunch, but they always work just inside the law and I can't catch them doing anything I can get them on."

Jace said, "Well,Justin, maybe me and my crew can help. I would like to put the two prisoners in your jail for a few days while we rest up. We have had a hard trip. I know Luther will be happy that he don't have to take care of them for a couple of days. We all could enjoy a little rest and a few good times. I think Luther needs the rest."

"Sure bring them in, and we will lock them up and go have lunch."

Jace went to the door and told them to bring the prisoners in. After they locked them up, Jace said, "Justin Barnes this is Fred Barlow, Hank Lassiter and Luther Anderson."

"Glad to meet you. I thought I was a pretty big man but that is the biggest man I ever saw."

They all laughed, "Yes,that Luther is a fair sized fellow."

"If you will wait while I go round up one of my deputies, we can go have lunch."

"Yeah, that sounds good," Luther said as he rubbed his stomach.

They went to the café and went in and sat down and the waitress brought cups and a pot of coffee. She announced, "The special is steak and potatoes and apple pie for desert."

They all agreed that would be fine. While they were waiting on their order,

Justin said, "I'm worried about you Jace I have heard that Lassiter has hired a new man and I think he is a fast gun. I don't know for sure but I have heard it is Kid Slade."

"I've heard of him. If it's him, he is very fast alright."

"What will you do if it is him?" Justin asked.

"I will try to avoid him but if I can't I will face that problem when I get to it. How did this man Lassiter get so much power around here?"

"He has a very powerful friend up in the Dakotas and he has a lot of pull in Washington."

"I don't care who he is he can't just run over everyone."

Justin shook his head, "I would love to put a stop to his crooked dealings but I have to operate within the law."

"I don't have to," Jace smiled. "But I don't want to get in trouble with you."

The sheriff said, "I'll cut you all the slack I can, but we'll have to be careful. I can tell you something else; he has a friend between here and Yuma that can be a lot of trouble too. His name is Tom Anderson and he has a couple of mean brothers too. He can cause us a lot of trouble if we have problems with Lassiter."

Jace frowned, "I don't think you need to worry about them any more because we had a run in with them and they are all dead. I needed to report that to you and take care of what ever we might have to face from the law."

"If you've taken care of that family, you won't have any problem from me. But you will probably have a lot of trouble from Lassiter and his bunch. That might be the reason for the new gun hand," Justin replied.

"Who is the friend he has in the Dakotas?" Jace asked.

"I don't know I have just heard rumors about this powerful friend. I think he has a lot of power in Washington."

"Well we will cross that bridge when we get to it."

Jace asked the sheriff, "Where's the telegraph office?"

"When you leave the café go toward my office turn left one block and you will see it on the corner."

"Thanks, I have some telegrams to send and I better get to it. Oh by the way do you know the Anderson place?"

"If you mean the Tom Anderson place yea I know where it is."

"Do you think it would be very hard for Jake Baker and his family to take it over?"

"No, we have a law in the state that if a place is left with no one to claim it you can do something like the homestead act and if any back taxes are due you have to pay them," Justin answered.

"Thanks, I'll talk to you later." He found the telegraph office, sauntered in, and told the old man he had some telegrams to send. The old man turned, spit a plug in the spittoon, and said, "Well, sonny that is what I am here for," and laughed

Jace smiled, "I guess so." He sent one to Fred Lawson and asks him if he could check on the law in Arizona about the Homestead Act and why he wanted to know then he sent one to Washington to General Lewis and asked what he knew about the Indian problem here with John Lassiter and then he sent one to Jennifer. He had a hard time trying to find the words to say to her because he knew he really liked her and he did not know how she felt about him and he knew that he had lost one love and he could not go through that again. He also knew that the reputation he had could cause a lot of problems for them. He sent that he thought about her quite often and he would really like to see her again.

The man asked, "Aint you Jace McCord?"

Jace answered, "Yes why?"

"well if it was anyone else going to send this about Lassiter I'd try to talk him out of sending this but you might be the one to get this town out from under his hold on everybody in town."

Jace said, "I thought you had a good sheriff?"

"Yea we do Justin is a good man but he has to go by the law and Lassiter is smart enough to follow the law when he is around the sheriff." "Well, I am not going to have any trouble with anyone in town if I can help it."

"Sonny, if you keep askin' questions about him you're going to have trouble with him as sure as I am standing here. He don't like anyone askin' about him or his business. Don't worry I wont let him know anything about your business I would like to see him get what is coming to him."

Jace left there and went to the Madison house and found that Fred had gotten him a room. They were all on the second floor and together. He went to his room and found all his gear that someone had put there for him. He was getting ready to see if he could get a bath when Fred and Luther knocked on his door.

He smiled, "You boys look mighty clean."

"Yeah, and we have a bath ready for you." Fred replied.

Luther said "Yea I want to be able to eat with out smelling like I am in a horse barn."

"If you wasn't so dog gone big I would take you down and rub your head in the floor," Jace laughed.

They all had a good laugh. Jace asked, "Where's Hank?"

"He is finishing his bath," Fred answered.

Luther said, "It sure is good to not have to worry about them prisoners for a while."

"Luther I want to tell you how I appreciate the way you have taken care of them while we have been on the trail."

"Wasn't know trouble."

"Maybe it wasn't any trouble to you but I don't know how we could have made it without you. You take care of those two like it is so easy. Without you it would take at least two men to watch those prisoners. Let's enjoy a few days here and then we will get started again. I want to find those two that Ricky told us about to help us take the prisoners on to Hays. Also I have to wait until I get a response to my telegrams."

Fred asked, "What about Lassiter and his bunch?"

"I'm not going to worry about them right now I just want a day or two to rest up for the trip home. I'm going to the four aces and have a drink and try to pick up some local rumors about this town and maybe find out what Lassiter is up to right now."

Hank asked," Care if I go with you. You might need some help."

"Yeah, I'll go, too, and I can help if you need it," Luther said as he jumped up from his chair.

"I appreciate the offer and I can't think of anyone that I had rather have with me in a fight but we don't need to look like we are there to cause trouble I just want to get some information if I can."

Jace and Hank left and he said, " hope we don't run into any trouble."

"Yea me to I just want a couple of days rest and be on our way," Jace replied as he patted the butt of his 45 colt.

"What if that general says you could help the Indians then what?" Hank asked

"I don't know but I can't just walk away and not help the sheriff and the Indians. I hate to see one man run the lives of so many that can't do anything about it."

"Yeah, but you can't save the whole country," Hank said.

"I know but the ones I can help make me feel that much better."

They walked into the saloon and stood in the door until their eyes adjusted to the darker room. They walked to the bar and the man in the dirty white apron and a dirty bar towel said, "What can I do for you?"

They ordered a beer and looked around the room. There were two tables with card games going on and three men stood at the other end of the bar. One of the men kept looking at them and Hank nodded his head down toward the men, "We may have trouble."

"I don't think so he looks like the one we are looking for. He wants someone to buy him a drink and will talk a lot about the town and the people."

The man was dirty and smelled like he hadn't had a bath in a long time He walked up and said, "Hi, you are new in town ain't you?"

"We just got into town and needed a cool drink," Jace replied.

The old man smiled through brown rotten teeth, "I sure could use a cool one myself."

"Bartender set up three more," As Jace pointed to the three of them.

"Thanks, mister, I don't find too many friendly people around any more, if you know what I mean?"

"I know what you mean. What is this town like? Is there any jobs around?"

"Well, it depends what kind of work you are looking for."Mr. Lassiter is always looking for good cowhands and I hear he is looking for men good with a gun. You look like you could fit that bill. You ain't no stranger to a gun"

"I don't hire out as a gun hand."

"Too bad," the old man said "Because you look like a man that could handle himself."

"What does this Lassiter need gun hands for?"

"Well, I don't know but the way I hear it he ain't gettin' any good gun hands. Seems like only cowboys and no good drifters. If I was you, I would not ask too many questions about Mr. Lassiter's business. He don't like people asking about him and his business"

"Thanks I will try to keep that in mind."

Two cowboys rode hard into the rocking L ranch and ran to the door and knocked on the door. The houseboy came to the door and said "May I help you?"

They said, "We need to talk to Mr. Lassiter now."

"Wait here, I will see if he is available." The boy answered

The boy returned and said "He will see you now."

He led them down the hall to a large room with a big desk. There were guns and animal heads all around the walls. Lassiter asked, "What can I do for you?"

One of the men very excited told him, "That gun hand you been waiting for is here in town."

"Are you sure it is him?" Lassiter questioned.

"Yeah, boss. It's him sure as shootin'."

"Well, we have someone to take care of him. I've heard he is pretty fast but I think Kid Slade is faster. I don't think anyone can stand up against Slade and live to tell about it."

One of the men shook his head, "I hope so boss because I've heard of the shooter and they say he's real good with a gun and I know some ole boys that went up against him and they ain't around anymore."

"Don't worry," Lassiter replied "Slade says he's faster and that's good enough for me. I'm going to wait and let him think about it for a while then I'll send Slade in to take care of him. You boys just stay clear of him till then because I don't want to loose any hands if I can help it."

"Well, boss, if you let me take four or five hands with me, you wont have to worry about him any more."

"Yea I would have five or six hands to burry. Men like McCord are dangerous and I don't need to loose any good hands to a man like that." Lassiter said.

"Well you sure don't have any faith in us do you?"

"Just leave him to me."

It was getting late and Jace said, "Let's go down to the café in the hotel and see how their food is."

Luther jumped up from his chair, "Yea food." And they all had a good laugh

When they started in the café the sheriff came in and they greeted him, "How about joining us for supper?"

While they were waiting for there order a girl brought a pot of coffee and cups for everyone. She said, "The special tonight is steak and potatoes gravy biscuits and coffee."

They all said that would be fine.

Justin looked worried, "Jace I think you better be careful I been hearing somc talk about this Kid Slade they say he is real fast with a six-gun."

"I've heard the same thing, but I am not going to worry till its time and now is time to eat."

Luther agreed, "I'm real hungry so lets eat then worry about problems."

Everyone had a good laugh about that and after the meal they went to the porch and sat and talked. Justin said, "I'll do all I can to keep trouble from startin',but I don't know what I can do to stop it if Lassiter is determined to go after you. I am no match for this Kid Slade but I will do what I can to stop him."

"No, don't do anything to get him to go after you because he'll kill you and never look back. If we have to deal with him I will take care of him."

"I could have some of my deputies help me and we could take him in and lock him up till this is over."

Jace ask, "Don't try, it because if he is as good as I think he is, he can take you and probably five or maybe even six of you. Just leave him to me if it comes down to it."

They all said good night and went to there rooms to get a good nights sleep. Jace opened his door and pushed it open and stood to the side just in case. Nothing moved so he eased in the room and lit the lamp. No one had been there since he put his things in there earlier. He put a footstool in front of the door just in case someone tried to get him during the night. He was tired and this was the first bed he has slept in for several nights. He got undressed and got in the bed and felt like he was going to sleep good tonight. He had a wild animal alert about him that he had developed over the years. Without it he would have been dead long ago. He hung his six-gun on the bedpost so he could get to it in a hurry in case he needed it. He did not know how long he had been asleep but he heard a scrape like a boot against the floor in the hall. He reached his gun and rolled off the bed. He waited what seemed like and hour but he knew it was just a few minuets. He heard the door latch move and the door eased open. He didn't think it was any of his bunch because they knew better than to slip up on him during the night like this. The door slammed open and someone fell over the footstool and someone else fired into the bed. He fired two quick shots at the muzzle flashes and heard a groan then the one that had tripped over the stool was getting up with his gun pointed toward the bed. Jace said don't try it mister but he fired and Jace shot him right between the eyes. He heard more footsteps down the hall and raised his gun to be ready but he heard, "Don't shoot it's me and Fred."

"Come on in."

They said, "What happened?"

"I guess someone was out to put me to sleep permanent." About that time he heard Justin coming down the hall saying, "What's going on in here?" "I don't know but I think your friend Lassiter just made the first move." They lit the lamp and Jace asked, "Do you know any of these fellers.?"

"No," Justin replied "But let me get Harry from the saloon and if anyone knows them he should."

It took him a while to get Harry there but he looked at them and said, "They were in the bar this evening and were talking about making some easy money. That was the first time I ever saw them."

"Well, thanks, Harry and sorry about getting you out so early."

"That's okay, sheriff I had just got into bed."

"Do you think Lassiter sent them to kill me?" Jace questioned.

"I don't think so I think it is just a couple of ole boys that figured to make some quick money. I don't think they knew who you were because they would not have attacked you if they really knew you. I will put someone outside to watch so you can get some sleep. Being sheriff is getting a little more active," and laughed.

"No I'll be fine. I don't want anyone getting hurt because someone is after me."

"Yea, but I don't want to have you on my mind because someone in my town killed you."

"I'll be alright just go back to bed and I'll see you in the morning."

"Okay," Justin replied. "I'll buy your breakfast."

"That's a deal."

Jace lay back down and couldn't go to sleep right away. Jennifer came to his mind and he found himself smiling. He really liked her but what kind of life could they have with the way he lived. He couldn't settle down and no one would look for him. Maybe I could hang up my guns and live a normal life. As soon as he said it he knew it was not true. Someone would always be looking to get the reputation of the man that killed the shooter. He didn't know what to do because to just walk away from Jennifer would be so hard. He would always remember her and how beautiful she was and how good he felt when he was with her. He finally went to sleep and woke with a start. He didn't know what woke him. He reached for his gun and listened for any sound. He heard footsteps in the hall and moved behind the door in case someone broke in. there was a knock at the door. He asked, "Who is it?"

" This is Fred are you awake we're going to breakfast."

"I will be right down," He must have slept more than he thought. It felt like he had just lay down and went to sleep. That was dangerous in a situation like this where someone is trying to kill him. He got dressed and went down stairs and met them. Justin wasn't there yet, but he said he would meet them there. They had ordered coffee and the waitress brought a pot of coffee and an extra cup like they ordered. They were just about to start ordering when Justin walked in.

"I am glad to see you alive and kicking this morning," Justin smiled.

"You are not the only one," Jace laughed.

While they were eating Justin said, "I talked to a couple of Lassiter's hands this most know the two men that attacked you last night. One of them said he heard them talking in the bar last night and all he heard was if they took care of something or someone that the big man in the country would be very grateful and pay them real good."

" Well that clears that up because if he had sent them I was going to have a talk with that gentleman about that."

After they finished eating Jace went to the telegraph office to see if he had any replies to his messages he sent. He had one from Gen Lewis in Washington. The message said will check into trouble in Phoenix .stop. if I find a problem will send someone to take care of it stop Gen Harry R Lewis U.S. Army.

He told the man at the office if he got any more messages please let him know. He said, "Yes sir I will send someone to notify soon as I get it."

Jace went back to the sheriff's office and talked to the deputy on duty.

"The sheriff is out of town but he'll be back around lunch."

"How are the prisoners doing?"

"They're fine. They had a visitor early this morning."

"Do you know who it was?"

The deputy answered, "It was one of Lassiter's men."

" Did you hear any of the conversation?"

"No," The deputy answered "They wouldn't talk when I was in the cell area with them but I can tell you they acted like they was very happy after that feller left."

"I wonder what's going on?"

"I don't know but I did hear Kid Slade's name mentioned."

"Well they must think that he will take care of me and their problems will be over. Tell them if they give you any trouble that I will send Luther down to take them the rest of the time."

He said, "Is that the big feller you had with you."

"Yea, that's him."

"Well, I'll tell them that should shut them up."

"If the sheriff gets back soon tell him I'll be around the hotel."

"I'll tell him, and Mr. McCord be careful because that Slade is meaner than a rattlesnake and can strike just as fast."

"Thanks I'll watch out for him, but I am not bad with a gun myself and call me Jace."

It was about 12:30 when the sheriff came to the hotel looking for Jace and said, "Something is up but I am not sure what."

"I know," Jace replied. "I feel just like I did in the war when something was about ready to happen. I'll be careful and you warn your deputies not to go against Slade or any other man Lassiter has hired. I will take care of them myself. I don't want anyone to get hurt because of this mess."

"Well," Justin replied "I think some of Lassiter's men are going to get hurt but I can't feel to bad about that."

"How about something to eat?" Jace asked.

"Sounds good to me." They walked in the café and found Luther, Fred and Hank all eating so they joined them and ordered.

Jace ask, "Justin do you know Rick Matson or Tim Rogers?"

"Yea. I know them why."

"Well a feller told me they were good men and I might get them to help us with the prisoners the rest of the way home."

Justin said, "They are both good men and I'll take you to meet them after we finish eating. I don't know if they would be willing to go with you but we can sure ask."

"Tim was found in the desert years ago we guessed that his family was killed by the Indians when they were coming out west. Rick's mother and father was killed when their wagon turned over and Rick and his brother was thrown free. I was always thought there was something funny about that. Lassiter wanted their spread and soon as they were killed he had it and I don't know how he got it."

After they finished eating they walked out to the front and sat in the benches and chairs. The hotel had on the front porch. They were talking about Lassiter when this young boy ran up and said, "Sheriff I have a message for Mr. McCord."

"This is Jace McCord, what's the message?"

" Mr. McCord the man said to tell you that you had a message at the telegraph office."

"Thanks son," Jace replied as he handed him a shinny quarter.

The boy said, "Thanks Mr."

"I'll see you later I am going to see what I have at the telegraph office." He walked in the office and the old man winked. "I have two messages for you sonny."

Jace said, "Thanks" and paid him. He walked outside and read the messages. One from Fred Lawson said I have checked and am sending the paper work for your friend to file on the land you told me about. Stop. If you need anything more let me know. Stop. The second message was from Jennifer. She said Dear Jace I will be so happy when you get home. Stop. I miss you so much and want to see you soon. Stop. Love Jennifer.

Jace stood looking at the message for a while and felt like he was floating on a cloud. He did not know how things would work out but he knew really liked this girl. He walked back to the hotel when a horse rode into town and the man got off and started toward him. He knew without asking who this was. The way he wore his gun the way he walked, this was the gunslinger Kid Slade..

He faced him and his hand automatically touched the butt of his gun in his holster. Luther and Fred walked out of the hotel and saw what was going on.

Jace yelled, "Stay back I'll handle this."

Fred said "Some of Lassiter's men are coming out of the saloon. We will keep them off you."

Jace faced Slade and waited. Slade said "I hear you are a big time gunfighter is that right?"

Jace stood there and didn't say anything. He learned from his Indian friends how to be still and quiet. Patience, it worked on the other man every time. by not saying anything made the other man mad and that was something a gunfighter couldn't afford..

"I heard you ain't nothing but a big coward," Slade sneered.

Jace just stood there and Slade was getting madder. Jace knew he had him where he wanted him because the gunfighters liked to make the man they were facing mad so they would loose their self control and not use their head.

Slade yelled, "You yellow boy that's what I hear. You better answer me boy or I am going to kill you."

Jace just stood quiet because he knew he had the best of Slade. He watched the gunslingers eyes and waited. He saw in his eyes that he was ready to draw. Slade made his move and Jace drew and fired. He felt something like a hot poker in his left arm and he could hardly stand. He saw Kid Slade go down and tried to raise his gun to shoot him one more time. Jace didn't want to shoot him again but he had to or be shot himself. He raised his gun when Slade dropped his gun and lay still. He heard more shots and turned and saw the men by the saloon go down and then he saw Fred fall. One of the men on the porch raised his gun to shoot Luther and Jace shoot him square in the chest. The rest of the men took off running. Jace ran to Fred and knelt down and held his head up. He said "Someone get the doctor."

"How bad is it?" Luther asked.

"I don't know," Jace replied. "But it don't look good."

Fred tried to speak but was too weak. Jace said, "Just lay still the doctor will be here in a minute."

The doctors said, "Take him to my office and you come and let me look at that arm."

Luther helped carry Fred to the doctor's office and when they got there Jace sat down and felt like he would pass out. Luther took a towel and put it in a pan of water and gave it to Jace. He put it on his forehead. It felt some better. He lay there for a while and he looked at Luther and saw he was crying he asked, "What is it?"

"Fred's dead," Luther told him.

Jace dropped his head," I don't know what to do I really liked him. I know one thing someone is going to pay for this."

"No," Luther said "Jace, we have been lucky so far. You beat Kid Slade and I never saw anything like it. I didn't see your hand move. Slade looked shocked when the bullet hit him like he could not believe someone could beat him to the draw. I saw the men on the porch make a move and Fred shot one of them and I got another one when Fred shot the next one I saw a man shoot him and I got him then you shot the next one. The rest ran like a pack of wolves."

" What happened?" Justin asked "I just got back."

Luther told him what happened and Justin said, "I never thought anyone could beat Slade to the draw and your friend, I am sorry about that he seemed like a very good man."

"He was fast alright and if he hadn't let his emotions take over I don't know if I could beat him or not" Jace answered " And yes, Fred was a good man and we will miss him."

"Where is Hank?"

Justin replied, "He went to get Rick and Tim so you could talk to them."

Jace nodded his head, "Good, I don't want anyone else getting hurt,. I'm going out to talk to Lassiter where does he live?"

"I will take you there," Justin replied"

"No," Jace said. "I don't want anyone else hurt. I just want to warn him if he starts any more trouble I will finish it for him."

Justin said "He won't take kindly to being warned. I think it would be best if I went. I could help in case of trouble and if you do have any trouble the law will be there."

"Okay, but be careful."

Hank and Luther said they were going.

" I don't need so many. The more we take the better chance we have of getting someone hurt."

Luther looked straight at Jace, "I'm going to go and the only you can stop me is shoot me."

Jace laughed, "Don't tempt me."

They rode out and he asked, "How far is his place?"

Justin told him "About five miles south of town."

They came over a large rise and looked down on a big two

story house with barns and corrals all around it. Jace was surprised. "This is a big place."

"Yes it is," Justin replied " But the way he got it was by hurting smaller ranchers and taking their land."

"I think he is about through," Jace sneered.

They rode up to the front of the house and a tall man with gray hair and beard walked out. He had two men by him and Justin said, "That's his foreman on the right and his helper on the left."

Lassiter yelled, "What do you want?"

Jace sat there for a while and Lassiter yelled, "State your business and get off my property."

Jace said, "I've' had enough of you Lassiter and if you don't shut up and listen you ain't gonna be able to do anything else."

Lassiter turned red and couldn't say anything for a minute. His face reddened "You can't talk to me that way. I will have you thrown off my place now get out of here."

Jace got off his horse and walked to the porch where they were standing, "You two backing this play?"

The foreman asked, "You the one that shot Kid Slade?"

"If it's any of your business, yeah, I shot him."

The foreman shook his head, "Mr.Lassiter, I can't go up against him. He killed Slade and we all watched him practice. If this man beat him, I can't come close to fighting him."

Lassiter started shaking and yelling,"You're fired now get your stuff and get out." The other man said, "Wait and I will go with you."

Lassiter looked toward the bunkhouse, "Who will stand by me?" No one moved.

He yelled, "If there was a man among you, you would help me take this bunch out."

One man yelled back, "Mr Lassiter we are cowboys not gun hands."

He turned red and yelled, "Get out, all of you, I don't need a bunch of cowards."

Jace walked to the porch and slapped him hard three times, "You had some good friends of mine killed and I should just shoot you, but I can't so I am warning you if you cause anymore trouble I will come after you." Jace started to get his horse and turned, "Oh, by the way I have a man from Washington looking into the Indian trouble that you've been causing so if I was you I would be happy with the land I had stole already and leave the Indians alone." He got on his horse and they rode back to town. No one said much on the way to town but when they got to town people were all standing in the street.

One man asked, "Well, what happened? How did it go."

Justin said, "You wouldn't believe it. Jace walked up to him and slapped him and told him if he caused any more trouble he would come after him."

One of the men in the crowd said, "I sure would like to have seen that. Mr. McCord, I sure would like to buy you a drink."

A lot more voices chimed in, "Yeah. me too."

Jace smiled, "I sure thank you, but I have to get ready we need to leave day after tomorrow. You shouldn't have any more trouble with him and if you do I will come back and take care of him."

They all cheered and told Jace he was welcome in their town and homes anytime.

"Thanks I hope to come back some time to visit you all, I better check the train schedule and see what time we can leave."

Justin was sad, "I am going to be sorry to see you all leave."

"We will be sorry to leave too, but I hope to come back sometime and see everyone again. By the way the army is going to check on the trouble here in case Lassiter tries anything."

"Thanks Jace this town and the Indians owe you a lot." Jace

got back from the station and Luther was hungry again. They all laughed and Jace told them,

"I think we can get something to eat." They ordered and were waiting for their food when Hank told Jace, "The two men I went to talk to said they would be here to talk to you this evening."

"Good did you like their looks?"Jace questioned.

"Yes," Hank replied. "They looked like good men." They had just gotten their food when three men walked in the café and came over to their table.

Justin said, "Jace I want you to meet Rick and Tim that I told you about."

Jace got up and shook hands with them and told them to sit down.

Rick replied, "Mr McCord I want you to meet my brother Ray."

Jace shook hands with him and they sat down. "Do you want something to eat?"Jace asked.

"Well we better not Mr McCord things haven't been to good to us lately," Rick said

Jace called the waitress over and told her, "Take their order and put it on my bill."

"Yes sir," and she left to get their orders.

"We will pay you back somehow," Rick told him.

"If you go with us this will be an advance on your salary, and if you don't just say I like to help when I can."

After they ate they went to the front and sat on the benches and talked. Jace told the Tim, Rick and Ray, Rick Baker said you might be interested in going with us and help guard the prisoners."

"Yea we would like that." Rick smiled.

"I have to warn you we have had a lot of trouble and lost two good men," Jace warned them.

“I would like to go with you but I can’t leave my brother here alone Mr McCord.”Rick told him.

“The name is Jace and I can’t pay him full salary but maybe I could go half or something like that.”

“That would be great Mr…I mean Jace.”

Ray grinned from ear to ear, “I would be happy with that, to get a chance to go with you and I will do my best to do my job.”

“Well I want you all to be very careful. I don’t want to loose anyone else. I don’t like losing good friends so you all be very careful.” Jace told them. “ We lost a very good friend this morning and one about a week ago and I don’t like it. I miss them a lot and will always remember them,” Luther stated.

“ We leave in the morning at 8:00 A.M. so don’t be late. We’ll have breakfast before we leave so see you then,” Jace told them and ask Justin if he could have the prisoners ready by then and he said “No problem they’ll be ready.”

“ Well I’ll be back to my babysitting job,” Luther said and they all laughed.

Jace laughed and told him, “You’re so good at it.”

They went to bed and get ready to leave early in the morning.

Jace heard a noise outside his door and he grabbed his gun and went to the other side of the door. A knock and he asked, “Who is it?”

“You ready to eat?” Hank ask

“I will be right down.” Jace said

Rick, Tim and Ray were there and talking to Luther. Jace told them, “You boys sure up early.”

“We slept on the benches on the front porch,” Tim replied.

“Why?” Jace asked.

Rick hung his head, “We didn’t want to be late and we didn’t have any place better to stay.”

“Well from now on you are going to have a better place to

stay. Lets eat and get ready to get the train loaded. "Rick, Tim do you have any horses you want to take?"

"No," They replied "Everything we have is in a sack and we're ready to go."

"Well the horse I have been riding is a good one and I am going to hang on to her. Luther and Hank have their own horses so we will have to load them and then get our gear loaded," Jace replied.

Justin walked in and said, "You boys are up and around early."

Jace rubbed his face, "We have a lot to do to be ready to leave on time"

"I sure am going to miss you all," Justin said.

They all said they would miss him too.

Jace ask Rick, "Do you have any guns?"

"No, they answered."

Justin replied, "When you come to get the prisoners I will give you all some guns. It is the least I can do for all you have done for this town."

"Thanks we appreciate that," Jace told him.

They talked and ate and enjoyed their time together. After they ate Jace said, "Luther take Rick, Tim and Ray to the jail and get the prisoners and the guns."

Luther told him, "Okay," and the four of them left to get the prisoners.

Jace went to the stable and picked up the horses and gave the boy at the stable an extra dollar because he took very good care of the horses. The boy said, "Thanks mister."

Jace laughed, "You did a good job and I think you deserve a reward."

The boy shook his head, "I like animals and I liked taking care of your animals because they are good horses."

Jace took the horses to the train station and tied them to the hitch rail and went inside. He ask the train master if the train was on time.

"Should be here any time now," the station master said.

He walked outside and met Hank there and he said, "I sure miss Fred and Les."

Jace agreed "I know how you feel. I didn't know them long but they were good men."

"I wish the man responsible would be punished" Hank thought out loud.

Jace said "I think he will be as soon as the army gets here."

They heard Luther telling the prisoners to shut up and keep moving. They came around the corner, "I sure will be glad to get rid of these two."

Jace laughed, " Me too."

"I didn't think we would see you again," Bart sneered.

"Well tough luck boys your boss man didn't have what it takes to get rid of me."

"Well if you beat Kid Slade I don't think nobody can stop you."

"Just keep that in mind when you decide to try to escape."

They heard the train whistle and Jace ask Rick and Ray to help him load the horses. They took the horses to the side of the station and waited for the train to stop. They went to the loading ramp for livestock and loaded them.

Rick said, "Jace if you need to help loading the prisoners we can handle this."

"Luther can take care of them but you can help get their gear loaded."

He asked Ray, "where are your things?"

"Tim has all our things," he replied.

Jace said, "When you get the horses loaded come on down and we will get settled."

Jace loaded their gear and waited for Rick and Ray. While he was waiting he thought about Jennifer and how much he was looking forward to seeing her again. He tried to get her off his mind because he knew he had no chance with her. She was so beautiful it was hard to keep from thinking about her.

Justin came up and said, "Must be something mighty important."

Jace looked up and asked, "What"

"You were a long way from here just then. Must be a girl you are thinking about."

"Well yes, someone I met before I left on this trip," He said "Justin could you do me a favor"?

Justin answered, "Sure just name it."

"I'll be getting some paper work from Hays about the land that Jake Baker wants to take over. I think Rick will be here soon and take care of the details. Tell Rick to send me a telegram about how they made the trip and how Jim is doing."

"Sure I would be glad to." Just then he looked and saw the Indians at the edge of town.

"Go get Billy Two Eagles" Justin told a young boy. There were about ten ponies just sitting there. The boy took off toward the sheriff's office and "I'm going to see if I can stall them until Billy gets here."

"Be careful they could be unfriendly," Jace told him.

"I don't think so they don't have any war paint on and they are not carrying very many weapons. Wait here and I will see what I can do," Justin told him. He started to the Indians and held his hand up in a sign of peace. They just sat there. Justin felt like running the other way but he kept going. Just about the time his nerves gave out he heard Billy talk to them in their own language. He felt better when the leader said something and smiled at Billy. Billy talked to them and they said something to him. Billy told Justin they wanted to talk to man who fights with fast gun.

Justin said, "Must be Jace they want."

He yelled and told Jace to come there.

He walked up and the leader told Billy something and Billy told Jace, "They want to tell you, you are honored in their tribe and would like you to be his blood brother You have done much for his people and you will be tribal warrior."

Jace agreed, "Tell him I would be honored to be his blood brother."

The chief took a knife and cut his hand and Jace did the same and they put their hands together and one of the other Indians put a piece of rawhide around their hands tying them together. The chief spoke in his language and chanted. Billy said they were now brothers of the spirit. They said something to Billy and he told Jace his name was White Hawk and was welcome in their teepee any time.

Jace said, "Tell him I am very honored and hope to visit his lodge sometime."

They bid each other goodbye and they rode away.

Justin laughed, "Boy that is a great honor."

"I know and feel very good about this. I think when the army gets this mess straightened out they will be Okay."

The train blew its whistle and they got ready to leave. Justin shook Jaces hand and said, "I don't know how to thank you enough."

Jace smiled, "Just come see me sometime."

"I will," Justin said "I have never seen any one as fast as you."

"I was just lucky."

Justin shook his head, "I don't think so."

The train pulled out and the waived good by and found their

seats. Luther had the prisoners in their seats handcuffed to the seat. Tim said, "Luther if you need some time away from them, I'll be glad to watch them for you."

"Thank you, I'll take you up on that sometime. You look big enough to take care of these two."

Jace watched the country go by and was thinking about Jennifer. He didn't know how he would work this out because he felt like someone would always be looking for him and she would be in danger but he knew he liked her and could never forget her. Maybe he would think of someway to tell her that he would not be good for her and get out of her life. He was so mixed up. He liked her so much but he knew she needed someone a lot better then he was. He thought when he delivered the prisoners he could just ride out and leave her alone and she could find a man that would make her happy. He would be happy to get rid of these two prisoners. He knew Luther would be glad to get rid of them. They would be in Hays in a few days and things would work out somehow. He would be sorry to see the friends he had made on this trip leave. He had become close to them and felt like they had been friends a long-time and not just a few weeks.

Jace walked to the platform between the cars and leaned on the rail and thought in a couple of days he would see Jennifer and he was happy but also he felt sad because he would have to tell her he was leaving and she would be better off with him gone. That's what he would do, he would deliver the prisoners and go somewhere and forget her.

Luther came out, "I'm sure glad to have Tim along. He don't mind staying with the prisoners. I can have a little time to just do what I want."

Jace smiled, "I'm sorry. I didn't think about you being tied down so much its just that I've had so much to think about."

"Hey, I didn't mean to say I was unhappy I'm just glad to have someone to help. I'm happy to be along with you all on this trip. I never had real good friends before and I really like the way I feel now. I have friends that I can joke and laugh with. It is good and I like you Jace. I have always been able to beat anyone around but with you I don't feel I have to fight you. Besides I could never match you with a gun."

Jace laughed, "Well that makes us even because I could never match you in hand to hand fighting. You are a very good man and I am happy to have you with me. You can ride with me anytime you want."

They talked for a while and Hank came out to get some fresh air. Luther said, "Thanks Jace for being my friend."

"Thanks for being my friend I hope we can always be friends."

Hank asked, "What was that all about?"

"I think everyone has always been afraid of Luther and he didn't have any friends."

Hank shook his head, "Yea that is pretty much how it was. Les and I tried to be friends with him but I think he didn't trust anyone until he met you. I don't know what you did but he likes you and trusts you a lot. I think he has even started trusting me more lately. Can I ask you something?"

Jace said, "Sure go ahead"

"Well I have noticed the closer we get to Hays the more you seem to pull away from everyone and I was just wondering if something was wrong?"

"Its nothing I have a problem to work out."

"Is it that girl you were telling me about? I don't mean to pry but I think of you as my friend and I would like to help if I could."

"Well I have to think about her. You know what kind of life I live and I'm afraid that she might be in danger if she's around me."

Hank said "I think you should talk to her and let her make up her own mind. I think she would be in less danger with you around than she would without you."

"I know I've tried to make all the reasons work about us being together. Another thing I don't know how she feels about me. I may not be what she wants."

Hank answered, "I feel like you really like this girl and you wouldn't be happy without her. I think what you've told me I am sure she likes you."

"I really like her. She is so beautiful and looking into her eyes makes me weak in the knees. I just want the best for her and not put her in danger because of me."

Hank told him, "Just wait till we get there and talk to her I think you will find out everything will be fine."

"Maybe you are right."

The man in the conductor suit came through and said dinner would be served in the dining car in thirty minuets. After they ate Jace sat back in his seat and closed his eyes and tried to take a nap but the rocking of the train would not let him go to sleep. He walked to the end of the car and watched the country go by.

Tim and Rick walked out and said, "Can we talk to you a minute?"

"Sure go ahead."

Tim acted nervous, "We had a pretty hard life there in Phoenix and you gave us a good chance to change things around and make something of ourselves. Nobody ever gave us a chance before and we just wanted to say thanks."

"Just do a good job and help us get these prisoners back to Hays and I will see you get a good chance to start with a real life, but you will have to work hard to make your lives what you want it to be."

Rick said, "We ain't afraid of work we just need a chance to do something on our own. Lassiter would not let anyone get ahead there because they might cut into his profits."

"Well you won't have to worry about anything like that here. There are some good people there and they will help you if you do for yourselves."

Rick stuck out his hand "I want to thank you too for talking my brother along. I couldn't go off and leave him there by himself. I have looked after him since our parents were killed and I guess I feel like I still need to look after him."

Jace shook his hand,"That's good but let him grow on his own too."

After all night on the train Jace thought he would be very happy to get to Hays. The porter came through and called for breakfast. They ate and talked for a while. The porter came through and said they would be in Santa Fe in one hour.

Jace told Hank that he was going to wire Fred Barlow and tell him they would be there sometime in the morning.

Fred told him, "I'll hold the train even if I have to lay in front of it."

Jace laughed, "I don't think that will be necessary. I'll be back in a minute."

Luther ask Tim if he would watch the prisoners for a little while so he could get off and stretch his legs. Tim said, "Sure go ahead I will keep an eye on them for you."

Someone called out all aboard and Luther came back on the train and ask Hank if Jace was back on yet. He said he hadn't seen him. He caught the porter and said we have someone that didn't make it back yet.

The porter told him, "I can't help it we have to keep on schedule."

Hank was just about to pull a gun on him when Rick said here he comes. They were yelling at Jace to hurry. He ran up the ramp and jumped and caught the last car just in time.

Tim said, "That was to close for comfort."

Hank told Jace he was about to pull a gun and hold the train till he got there.

Jace frowned, "Don't do that I would hate to break you out of jail."

They all laughed and got ready for the long ride to Hays. The day passed pretty well and after supper Jace went to the platform between the cars to get a little fresh air. The air was cooler now that they were getting out of the desert. The rest of the trip was long and tiresome but it was just about over. The porter came through calling Hays next stop.

Jace asked "How long before we get there?"

He answered, "About one half hour."

Jace ask Rick and Tim to go with Hank to get the horses unloaded and Luther would take care of the prisoners. "I'll get Ray to help with their luggage and meet them at the station."

Rick nodded, "Ok we'll take care of that and meet you as soon as they can get unloaded." The train started slowing. Jace and Ray took the bags to the nearest door. Luther was there with the prisoners waiting for the train to stop. They pulled up to the loading platform and Luther took the prisoners off. Jace and Ray unloaded their gear and was looking toward the stock car. Hank came off first with a horse and Rick and Ray followed with the rest of the Jace heard someone calling his name and looked down toward town and saw Jennifer coming toward him calling his name. He didn't remember how beautiful she was. He watched her and thought how much he really cared for her but he could not let that happen because she would be in to much danger by being close to him. She ran to him and jumped in his arms and kissed him long and tender. He felt like his legs were going to give out. He couldn't stop shaking. She felt so warm and wonderful in his arms. He thought I will not have the strength to leave her if I don't get out of here soon. She felt so good in his arms and he never wanted to let her go. When she kissed him it was like there was no one else in the world.

She held him close, "I've missed you so much. I have been so worried about you because daddy said you were in danger because some one was trying to stop you and he didn't know why."

Jace said,"We need to have a long talk as soon as I get everything unloaded and the prisoners in jail."

She asked, "Is anything wrong?"

"I just need to talk to you."

She looked so sad, "Ok but make it soon because I am worried that something is wrong."

"I'll hurry."

Sheriff Ben Anderson met them and Jace introduced him to everyone.

Ben said, "lets get them to jail."

"Fred Lawson wants to see you in his office as soon as possible."

Jace told Ben, "Luther will help with the prisoners until you get them locked up."

Ben smiled, "He don't look like he needs any help."

Jace laughed, "You're right he can pretty well take care of himself."

Jace told everyone to meet at the Hays rooming house and get rooms for everyone and he would meet them as soon as he could.

He opened the door to Fred Lawson's office and Hailey his secretary greeted him. "Hello Mr. McCord."

He said, "Jace please Mr. sounds to official and I am just a plain old country boy."

"Well Jace Mr. Lawson will see you in just a minute. I know

Jennifer was glad to see you that is all I heard while you were gone."

Just then Fred Lawson and another man came out and Fred shook the mans hand and looked at Jace, "Well hello Jace I was getting worried about you. I heard about all the attacks on you. Do you have any idea who was behind them?"

"I think it has something about the two men I brought back."

Fred told the other man, "Joe I will talk to you later right now I have some important business to take care of."

He took Jace in his office and shut the door, "Sit down and lets talk. I know you need some rest but I need to know something."

"Well if I can help I will be happy to."

Fred was nervous, "I just wanted to ask how you felt about Jennifer I don't want her to get hurt and you are all she can think about. If you don't feel the same way I need to know."

"Well Fred to tell you the truth I care for her very much but I am afraid she would be in danger with me. You know my reputation and with all the young guns looking to make a reputation they will be looking to fight me and be the one that took out Jace McCord and I fear for Jennifer."

"You just told me what I wanted to know. I think you are in love with her and I know she is in love with you. Jace I want you to think about the first day you saw her. You didn't know her and she was in a great deal of danger. I think she is safer with you than without you and I know what she will tell you. She will take the chance with you because she will be better off with you than without you. I want you to know I would not take a chance with my daughter if I felt like she was in great danger. I feel better with you around her because she couldn't be any safer.

Tell the friends of yours that helped you I will have their money ready as soon as I can contact the board and get the voucher. Tell them that I will make arrangements at the hotel and the café."

Jace said, "I told Rick that I would try to get half pay for his brother because he didn't want to leave him alone. I think most of them are going to stay around here. If you know of any jobs I am sure they would be interested."

Fred replied, "I need to talk to Jennifer and Jessica but I think they would like for you all to come to supper tonight. Jace don't worry about Jennifer I don't think you will be able to convince her that you are wrong for her."

"I don't want to put you and your family out but if you and the girls want all of us there we would be very happy to eat with you this evening. I am sure the boys would like something good to eat for a change."

"Jace I think Jennifer is going to want you to be there. You are all Jessica and I have heard about all the time you were gone."

Jace said, "I'll tell the boys and tell them to clean real good."

They laughed and Fred said, "We will see you about seven this evening."

"Sounds good see you then."

Jace went to the hotel and found the room they had for him and told the clerk that Fred Lawson would be making arrangements for their rooms. The man said that will be fine.

Jace thought out loud, "We may as well eat here too so he won't have to make arrangements all over town."

He went to his room and was putting his things down when there was a knock at the door. He pulled his gun and stood behind the door. He asked, "Who is it?"

"Its us,"Hank replied "We wondered how we were going to pay for these rooms."

Jace opened the door and let them in, "Fred Lawson said he

would take care of everything until he got the money to pay you all for helping me and by the way Ray he said he was going to pay you the same as the rest of us for the trip."

Rick looked away for a minute, "He must be a good man to do that. We ain't used to being around someone like that."

"I told him I thought some of you might like to stay around here and if he found any jobs let us know."

They all said they wanted to stay here and work and make a good life for themselves. He told them about the supper and they were all invited.

Tim and Rick said, "We can't go."

Jace asked, "Why?"

"We don't have any clothes to wear to some place like that. What we have on is the best we have."

"Come on with me we will take care of that." He took them to the store and told them to pick out something to wear. They took a pair of jeans and a wool shirt each. Jace said, "Here let me help you." He picked out a nice set of clothes for each one and told them to keep the shirt and pants they had picked out.

Rick rubbed his eyes, "I don't know what to say I never had anyone help us like this."

" Well from now on you are all going to have it better. Lets go get some lunch."

they all agreed Jennifer walked in her fathers office and Hailey smiled, "Hi Jennifer your father is in go on in. I saw Jace today he is so good looking."

Jennifer said "He sure is and I have never felt like this for anyone else. He makes me so happy when I am around him and I want to be with him all the time."

Hailey looked at her, "Sounds serious"

"I don't know he was so cool toward me today when the train arrived. I don't know what to think now. I will talk to you later I need to see daddy."

She went into the office, "Hi daddy I want to talk to you if you have time."

"Sure honey sit down. What is thc trouble you look like you lost your best friend."

"Daddy I feel like that too. I thought when Jace left that he really liked me but today when he arrived at the station he was so distant."

"Honey hold on I think there is something you need to know. He told me today that he cared for you very much but was so afraid for you because of his past."

She said, "I don't understand what does that have to do with us."

"He thinks someone will always be looking for him to prove they are better with a gun than he is and that you might get hurt."

"That is not true if anything I am safer with him than without him."

"That's what I told him. I ask him and his new friends to come to supper tonight do you and Jessica mind?"

"No we will be happy to fix dinner for them. I know Jessica will be glad to help too."

"I told them seven" "That will be fine. I will be so happy to see Jace now that I know what the trouble is. I was worried that he didn't like me."

Jace finished eating and told the rest of them to look around town and he would meet them back at their rooms in an hour.

Luther asked, "Can I go with you I think you are going to the jail to check on the prisoners." "Sure come on"

Tim said, "I'd like to go with you if you don't mind."

"Sure come on we are just going to the jail and see if everything is all right."

They opened the door to the sheriff's office and met Ben Anderson sheriff of hays.

Jace greeted him, "I just wanted to check on the prisoners."

Ben said, "Come on in I want to talk to you." They sat down and he said "Have you ever heard of Sam McMurtry of the bar eight ranch up in the Dakotas?" "No," Jace asked. "should I?"

"Well he's a very powerful rancher and is big in politics. These two boys in jail are his sons. He is also kin to that John Lassiter the man you had trouble with in Phoenix."

"You don't think that he is who has been trying to stop me on this trip do you?"

"I not only think so I am almost sure. That's something like he would do to get his sons back. A couple of years ago he killed a sheriff and two deputies's to break his boys out of a jail in Kansas. He didn't do the killing but some on his gunmen did and it was never proven but everyone suspects he was behind it."

Jace nodded, "What do you want to do?"

"I'll hold them till the trial and they will have to face what ever the judge gives them."Ben replied "I will swear in some more deputies to help during this time."

Luther and Tim both spoke up, "Sheriff we would be happy to help."

"Ben you couldn't get any better than these boys If you need more I think some of the rest that helped me get them here will be glad to help."

"Are you sure?" Ben asked. "Because it could get pretty rough. I used you Luther a while ago. I told them if they didn't settle down I was going to get you "

They all laughed.

"Sure we will help and be happy to."

Jace replied, "I'll help but I am going to be busy for a while. If you need help let me know and I will be here for you."

"I'll take your help anytime Jace."

Jace asked, "How long do you think we have before they try anything?"

Ben said, "I don't know but I think they will have to get Sam's Okay to do what ever they are planning and I think we have a couple of days to get ready. You and the boys that helped you need some rest so take tomorrow to rest and then we can get ready."

Jace smiled, "We'll be ready."

He told Luther and Tim they had better get ready to go to Fred's house to eat.

Luther rubbed his hands together, "I am ready now."

Jace laughed, "I don't think the girls know what they are getting their selves into."

They met the rest of their friends back at the hotel. Jace told everyone, "Lets get ready to go and we can meet down in the lobby when you are all ready."

Hank nodded, "You know that girl that met you today at the train sure is pretty."

Rick smiled and said, "She sure acted like she was glad to see you too."

Jace turned red, "You know I can leave you all here and go by my self."

They all laughed, "We'll be good. We promise."

They all met in the lobby and were ready to go. Rick said, "You know I don't think we have ever felt so good and been dressed so good before. I think you have some very good friends here Jace. I hope we can stay here and make good friends."

"I think it is up to you, if you want to stay here and to make friends it's your choice. I think you will do good here and you're good men. You will have good friends. Well lets go eat."

Luther stood up, "That's what I've been waiting for."

They walked the three blocks to Fred's house and knocked on the door. Fred met them and said, "Come on in. We are happy to have you all here."

Jace said "Fred I don't think you have met all these men."

He introduced them and they went to the living room and Fred told them to sit and make themselves comfortable.

Rick spoke, "Mr. Lawson we sure thank you for helping us with clothes and this time with your family and all you have done for us."

"The name is Fred and I should be thanking you for helping bring the prisoners back. I know you may not know it but you were all in great danger."

Just then Jennifer and Jessica came in the room. Jessica went to Jace and took his hand and smiled, "I am so glad to have you here."

Jace introduced every one and the girls greeted them, "Come on and sit at the table we are just about ready to eat."

They sat down and the girls put the food on the table and Fred gave thanks for the food and that the men were here safe after the long dangerous journey. They started to pass the food and Luther spoke, "I don't think I ever saw so much good food in my life."

"You've never met anyone like Luther he can eat like no one I ever met but also I never met anyone as good and would stand by a friend no matter what. I think all these men I met on this trip are the best I ever ran into." Jace stated.

Jennifer sat next to Jace and she would touch his hand and smile at him all through dinner. After they ate Fred told everyone, "lets sit on the porch, I would like to talk to you all."

They sat on the swing and some chairs on the porch. Fred said, "I talked to Ben today and he told me about the prisoners and who they were. He also said some of you told him you would help as deputies if he needed them. He said he would be very happy to have your help. I think you need to know that it could be very dangerous and I don't want you going into something without knowing what is ahead of you."

They all said, "We will all help if he needs us and we will be happy to do whatever it takes to keep this town safe."

In the kitchen Jessica asked, "Did you see the one they called Ray."

Jennifer laughed, "I saw all of them but I think he is the only one you saw."

Jessica blushed, "He has such pretty eyes and he is so nice."

Jennifer told her, "You don't know anything about him."

"Jace likes him so he must be a good man."

"But Jessica he likes him as a man to work with. How he would be as someone to fall in love with would be something else."

Jessica snapped, "I didn't say I was going to fall for him besides a look at you, you fell for Jace the first time you met him."

"I did not but you are right I did fall for him and didn't know to much about him. I just know he is the only one I will ever love. I feel so good inside and so safe when he is around."

"Maybe you feel that way because he saved you."

"You know Jessica daddy said the same thing but it is not true. I just know I am only happy when he is with me and so lonely when he is away."

Jennifer and Jessica finished the dishes and they came to the porch and Jennifer said "Jace come with me."

Fred told the men, "We are through but you men remember what I told you and be careful."

Jennifer led Jace out the front and down toward the river. She said, "I just wanted some time with you. I haven't seen you since you got back." They walked to the river and she turned and kissed him. He held her close and felt like he was going to float off. He had never felt like this before. When she kissed him it was like nothing he has ever felt before. Her soft warm breath on his lips and she was so soft and warm to hold. He looked into her eyes and told her, I fought this but I am in love with you. I will just have to make sure you are always safe."

She held his face in her hands and kissed him, "I love you more than I ever thought possible."

He held her close and looked deep in her eyes, "I am so afraid something may happed to you because of me and my life."

"Jace listen to what I feel first and know I love you and don't ever want to be without you."

"I know but…"

She stopped him and said, "I know what you are feeling because dad told me, but you have to know how I feel. I feel safer with you than I ever did without you. The day I met you I was in more danger than I have ever been in my life and I didn't know you then and you saved me. You save me every time you touch me. I have never felt like this before about anyone and when you kiss me I feel like I will fall down because my knees are so weak."

"I do love you Jennifer I tried to say I didn't but I know that I do. On that trip you are all I could think about and tha's why I want you to be safe and not have me put you in danger because of my reputation."

"I know I want to be with you and safe or in danger, good times or bad times I only know I want to be with you."

He looked at her and knew this was the most beautiful girl he ever seen, and he loved her more than anything else in the world. He took her in his arms and kissed her and felt like nothing he had ever felt before. He knew he would have to make sure she was always safe no matter what.

They sat on a bench that was in a park by the river and she said, "Tell me about you and what your life has been like."

"Not much very interesting about me,"Jace answered

"Let me be the judge of that," She said. "What about your family do you have any brothers or sisters?"

"I had one brother and one sister but I don't know where they are. When I came home from the war everyone was gone and I couldn't find them.. I looked for a long time trying to find some trace of them but I didn'

t find a clue to where they were."

She ask, "What was the war like?"

"It is hard to talk about but I was very young when I joined up and was scared all the time. I met an old man in our outfit and he taught me many things about staying alive and honor and courage and just about every thing I needed to know. He told me if I wanted to stay alive I needed to learn to shoot. I guess I took him serious because the next battle I found a dead soldier and he had a six gun and holster and I took I from him. I felt bad but I needed to learn to shoot and all I had was a musket so I took the gun and practiced with it all the time. That is where I got the name shooter. The boys in my company teased me about shooting so much and started calling me shooter. I practiced all the time and I guess I got pretty good. My friend told me one day I was the fastest he ever saw and not only that I was good at hitting the target. I was very close to that old man and when he got killed in a battle I thought I would never get over it. That's why I am afraid to be with you. My wife Karen and my daughter were killed and seams like every time I get close to anyone I loose them and I couldn't stand to loose you. I loved my wife and was happy with her but I never felt like I do with you. I loved our baby girl and I thought I would loose my mind after they were taken from me. I know if I ever lost you I wouldn't be able to stand it because I love you more than I ever loved anyone else."

Jennifer told him "I am so happy you told me all this because I understand more now. This morning when you told me we needed to talk I thought you didn't care for me and I would loose you. Now I understand what was wrong and that you really do love me. I can't say what will happen but I do know all the time we have together will be wonderful and I will be happy for as long as we have together."

He kissed her and told her he would die before he let anything happen to her.

"Jace, please don't talk about anything happening to you. I don't know what happened but I have fallen so deep in love with you and I want a long happy life with you."

They looked into each others eyes and knew they would always be together.

"Jace did you see Jessica and Ray look at each other this evening?"

Jace smiled, "I thought they were looking at each other a lot."

"She told me that she really liked him. Do you think he is Ok and it would be all right for her to like him?"

"I don't know but I do know he is a good boy and I think she would be alright if she liked him. I'll keep watch and make sure he doesn't hurt her. We better get back before Fred comes looking for us."

She said, "I think he is happy I am with you and he doesn't worry about me like he did when I was out with other boys. He said I was safer with you than with anyone else he could think of."

"Before we go I want to tell you something. I don't know where to start but I do love you. I have a ranch in New Mexico and I would like to go there someday and build it back to a good working ranch. I don't know how you would feel about moving that far away."

"I would go anywhere you went because I love you and want to always be with you." "I need to check on some things before we plan anything. I don't know how this thing with the prisoners is going to work out. I don't think their father is going let them stand trial for murder without trying something. I know it is going to be dangerous and I want you safe."

"I will be alright but I don't want anything to happen to you,"She told him

"I can pretty well take care of myself if I don't have to worry about you."

"Don't worry about me I will be safe," She replied.

"We better get back to your house."

"Just a minute," She said. "And she kissed him so soft and wonderful.

He didn't know if he could stay on the ground. He told her"I feel so good when you kiss me. Just being with you is better than anything I ever known before."

The next morning they met for breakfast and talked about what might happen if someone tries to break the two men out of jail.

Luther said, "I think I need to hang around the jail just in case anyone tries anything."

"Ok," Jace said "But if you run into anyone that looks like a gunman promise you will come and get me."

"Ok I will" he promised.

Tim remarked, "I think I will hang around with Luther just in case he needs help."

They finished eating and Jace said, "I have some things I need to do but I will be around town if you need me."

Rick and Ray said they would look after the horses and walk around town to see what was here and keep an eye on things also. Jace left them and went to the telegraph office and sent a telegram to an old friend of his in New Mexico to check on his land.

In the message to Haven Honeycutt taos New Mexico how is ranch. stop. Will be there sometime in the near future. Stop. Hope everything Ok with you and family. Stop. Jace McCord Hays, Kansas.

Jace walked back to the sheriff's office and found Ben there.

Ben nodded, "Sit and have a cup of coffee."

"Thanks I think I will," Jace replied "Have you heard anything about the prisoners?"

"Nothing yet. I sure would like it if Jim Harrison was still marshal here. The man that is marshal now we can't count on in case of trouble."

Jace said, "I think we have enough help that we can handle anything they send our way."

"I hope your right I heard about a gunfighter in Topeka that is headed this way."

Jace ask, "Do you know his name?"

"I think it is Seth Thompson you ever heard of him?" Ben asked.

"Yea I have and I hear he is pretty fast."

"I think he is real fast and I hope he is not headed this way because I don't have anyone to stop him," Ben told him

"I don't think he is going to bother us but if he does come this way promise to call me when he comes to town. I know he is a faster gun than most average men but I am pretty fair with a gun myself."

"I remember the day you saved Jennifer and how fast you were. I never saw anyone move as fast as you did. Well we'll worry about that when the time comes. He is probably just passing through and won't bother us," Ben answered.

"I have to go but if you need me I will be around."

"Luther and Tim are around here somewhere," Ben said "They came in earlier and said they would be close by in case of trouble."

"Ben they are good men but they are no-match for a gun hand like this Thompson, so call me if you see someone like that. I'll see you later Ben take care now."

Jace went back to the hotel to change his shirt and go see Fred about the file on the land for Jake Baker and his family. He walked into Fred's office and Hailey said, "Good morning Mr. McCord."

"Please just Jace."

"Sorry Mr. I mean Jace. Mr. Lawson will be with you in just a minute."

"That's fine. I am in no hurry."

"Jace the men that came with you are they pretty good men?" Hailey asked

"I think so I like them. They are sure enough men to have with you in a fight."

She smiled, "He sure is a big man isn't he?"

"Who do you mean?"

"I don't know his name but he is so big," Hailey replied

"You must mean Luther?" Jace asked.

"I didn't know his name but he sure is a good-looking man and so big."

"He is big all right. I am just glad he is on our side," Jace smiled.

"Is he married or anything?" She questioned.

"No would you like to meet him?"

"No, I would be afraid he wouldn't like me and don't want him to think I was too forward."

Jace told her," He is really a good man. I think he would like you just fine and I can make it seam like it was my idea for you to meet."

"I am afraid but I would like to meet him."

"Don't worry about it I'll take care of it" Jace told her.

Fred came in, "Hello Jace come on in I want to talk to you."

They went into his office. "Sit down. I have a couple of jobs if some of your friends want them. By the way what was that you and Hailey were talking about?" Jace laughed, " Hailey was asking about Luther. It seams like she has eyes for him."

"Oh good now I am going to lose my secretary." Ben smiled. "I'll tell the boys about the jobs but right now I am worried about the prisoners and maybe we need to keep everyone handy for a while."

"I think maybe you're right. Those jobs will be there for a while. I also received a telegram from Santa Fe and your friend Ricky Baker said tell you that they filled on the land and the judge said it looked good. They would probably get it soon and some of the ranch hands wanted to stay on with them when they took over. He also said he was going to have a new brother-in-law and said you would know what he meant."

"That is great news," Jace smiled.

"Oh by the way he also said that the army arrived and the major in charge of the area had been relieved and a new commander had taken over. I guess that is good news."

"It sure is." Jace told him

Fred said, "I want to tell you that my daughter is in love with you, so if that is not what you want please stop it before she gets hurt too much."

"Don't worry we talked last night and I think we are going to be all right because I know I can't think of being without her. I will just have to make sure she is safe and no one can hurt her."
"I just want you to know that Jessica and myself are very happy about you and Jennifer. I meant to ask you also what do you know about this boy Ray? He is all she has talked this morning and I worry about her."

"I think he is a good boy. Him and his brother have had a hard life since their parents were killed. I do know he will stand by you when the chips are down and I think that is the best way I know to judge a man."

"I hope so, she sure seams to like him," Ben told him. "I am just glad I only have two girls. Now I have to worry about my secretary. I guess it is good that everything is happening to fast. Well I don't think there is anything I can do about it so I won't worry about it now."

They all met back at the hotel and had supper and talked about the day they had. Tim joked, "Ray's it seams like you couldn't keep your eyes off that pretty girl when we ate last night."

"What do you mean?" Ray asked.

"You know who we mean little brother, "Rick said

He turned red and didn't know what to say. They laughed and Ray said, "She sure is pretty but I wouldn't have a chance with someone as beautiful as she is."

"Don't sell yourself short," Jace said. "I think she likes your looks too."

"You really think so?" Ray asked very excited.

"I sure do." Jace laughed. "But you be sure about her because I would very unhappy if she got hurt."

"I'd never hurt her. In fact I'd get anyone that tried to hurt her," Ray told him.

They finished eating and went to their rooms and tried to get a good nights sleep. Jace lay awake and thought about Jennifer and wished he could have seen her before he went to bed. Well he had so much to think about but he finally went to sleep. When he woke it was almost daylight. He dressed and went downstairs to the dining room for breakfast. He had just ordered when the rest of the crew walked in. they ate and talked for a while.

Luther told Jace, "Tim and me are going to the jail and hang around for a little while."

Hank said he was going to find a barber and get a haircut and Jace told him where it was. They decided to meet back here at noon.

Jace was sitting on the front porch of the hotel when a young boy came up to him and ask if he was Mr. McCord and he said he was. The boy said the man at the telegraph office wanted to see him. Jace gave the boy a quarter and said, "Thanks."

He went to the office and the man said he had a reply from the message he sent yesterday. It was from Haven Honeycutt she said his ranch was a little run down but she would send her two nephews Jordan and Larry to get things in a little better shape. She was glad he had gotten himself straightened out and was coming home. He took the telegram and went to see Jennifer. He knocked on the door and Jessica answered the door.

"Hi Jace, come on in and I will get Jennifer," Jessica said.

She went upstairs and came down in a minute, "Jennifer will be down in a little while. Where are your friends?"

"If you mean Ray, he's helping his brother with our horses."

She blushed, "Well he is the one I was wondering about."

Jennifer came down and went to him and kissed him, "I am so glad to see you I missed you last night."

"I know but until we get the trail over I don't think things are going to be normal around here."

She said, "lets go to the porch swing and talk." "Bye Jessica's I will see you later."

"Bye." She said, "Tell Ray I would like to see him."

"Ok," He replied.

They sat in the swing and he said "I want to show you something." and pulled out the telegram and showed her.

"Is it a good ranch?" She asked.

"It was before I left. But it is a little run down now. I have a friend looking after it but she has a ranch of her own to look after so it needed a little fixing up right now."

"How large is you ranch?" She asked.

"A little over 7000 acres," He replied.

She sat for a little while before she spoke, "I never thought it was that large."

"Well in New Mexico that is not too big. I know of places in southern New Mexico and Texas much larger than that."

"I have thought a lot about your ranch since you told me about it. I dreamed that someday I may live on it and be your wife. I know that is silly but you know how girls like to dream. I think it would be wonderful to be married to you. I have never thought that about anyone else. You are the most wonderful, special man I ever met. I couldn't think of anyone like you before. You are my dream come true."

"My wife Karen's father left it to us before he passed away. It was to big for me to take care of by myself. We didn't have the money to hire extra help. We had seven men working for us but it was to much for them also."

"It sounds wonderful and I would love to see it."

"I hope you can soon, "He told her.

Just then a boy ran up and said, "Mr. McCord the sheriff wants to see you as soon as you can get there."

"Ok," He told the boy and pitched him a coin.

"Jennifer go to the house and keep Jessica in there too until you heard from me or your father."

"Okay, "She said and ran to the house."

Jace ran to the sheriff's office and asked, "What's wrong?"

Ben met him at the front door, "That gunfighter we were talking about is here and said he is taking the two prisoners out and taking them home."

"You mean Seth Thompson?" Jace asked.

"That's the one," Ben replied.

Luther and Tim were there and Ray, Rick and Hank all came running up about then.

Jace said, "You all stay out of this. I don't want anyone getting hurt. He's very good with a gun but I think I can beat him. If he has anyone with him just keep them off me because I can't worry about anything else and face him."

They said they would. Just then he heard someone call his name. He looked around and in the street was a man that new how to handle a gun. You could tell by just looking at him.

" McCord, I'm talking to you. I come to get Mr. McMurtry boys out of jail so you just stand out of the way and I'll get them and no one gets hurt," Called the man in the street.

Jace told everyone to stay there and he stepped into the street. He faced the gunman and stood there. Seth said, "You are fast but I am faster."

Jace stood and didn't say anything. He was thinking about Jennifer and how much he loved her but he could not think of anything like that and live so he cleared his mind and said "If you're not the hang man you can't have them."

He said, "we'll see about that. This is between me and you or are your friends going to join in?"

"What about your friends?" Jace asked. "Are they going to join in or just the two of us?"

Seth said, "No I want the pleasure of taking you myself."

Jace was alert and watching his eyes to catch his play for his gun. He saw the look in his eyes and went for his gun. Seth had his gun clear but had not brought it to his target when he felt something hit him in the chest and he didn't know what happened because no one could beat him to the draw but his gun fired into the ground and he was falling. Then every thing was over for Seth Thompson. Jace spun his gun and dropped it in his holster. He looked at the five men standing there that had been with Seth Thompson and said, "Which one wants to be next?"

They stood there, "We ain't no match for you."

"Well go for your guns or get out of here." Jace smiled as he told them.

They started to turn when a big man said, "I Can't match you with a gun, but if you put your gun down I will tear you apart."

Jace told his friends to watch the rest of them and he took off his gun belt and hung it on a rail and started to the street. Luther said "I think I should get a chance to do my share you already took care of one of them so I should get to have my chance."

"I can take care of myself, Luther," As Jace smiled at him.

"I know you can Jace but I want to have my fun too," Luther said smiling back at Jace.

Luther walked to the street, "Come on I'll fight you."

He said, "I want to fight that guy that shot our friend."

"You're going to fight me and like it." It made the big man mad and he came at Luther with fists as big as hams. Luther stepped aside and tripped the man and turned ready to meet the next attack. The man got up and ran at him trying to hit him and throw him off balance. Luther hit him in the gut and the man went down gasping for air. He stood up trying to get his breath back. This time he took a stance and faced Luther ready to fight him. Luther was ready for him. He stood his ground and had his hands ready. The big man swung at him and grazed his shoulder. Luther hit him a glancing blow to the shoulder but it almost knocked him down. The man shouted "look out" and Luther looked behind him and too late figured he had made a mistake. The big man hit him on the jaw and almost put him to the ground. Before he could get his balance, the man hit him in the gut. He had to catch his wind before the man could hit him again. He backed up and held his hand up to protect himself. He saw the man come at him and he acted like he was still groggy and when the man came in reach Luther brought his right fist up and caught the man squarely on the jaw. He knocked the big man back and he hit him hard and fast to the gut and head until the man went down. He looked up at Luther and said, "I ain't never been whipped before but it ain't no shame. You are the biggest man I ever saw. I thought I was big but beside you I am not as big as I thought."

Luther reaches down and took the man's hand and helped him up. He said, " How come you are mixed up with this scum?"

"I was riding into town and stopped at the saloon to get a drink when they ask me if I would like to earn ten dollars. Man I ain't had that much money in a long time. They said all I had to do was if they had to fight I was to whip all I could take on."

Luther told them, "My name is Luther what is yours?"

"Steve Axton," He replied.

He took him to Jace and introduced them and Steve said, "I never saw anyone as fast as you. I thought I had seen some fast guns before but nothing like you."

"You just need to pick your friends better," Jace said

"I know," Steve replied. "I will from now on. It's just that I was hungry and ten dollars sounded good."

"You boys want to draw against me or are you leaving?" Jace asked.

"Why we got to leave that big man is gettin to stay?" One of the men wanted to know.

One of the other men said "We are leaving I ain't gona' try to draw again you. I watched ole Seth practice and I thought no one could beat him and you did so I am gona get out of here. If ole John wants to stay and face you that's up to him."

John shook his head, " No, I am going with you." They all left town pretty fast.

Ben Anderson came over to Jace and said, "Well I guess they won't try that again."

"I'll keep my guard up. I don't think they are through. McMurtry is not going to stop until he has his boys out of jail. We need to get Luther and Steve fixed up they look a mess," Jace said

Ben said, "Maybe you are right I will keep watch. Here bring them into my office and we can get the doc here. Call the undertaker and tell him he has a customer here at the jail."

Fred led the way to his office and they went in. Jace pointed to a chair "Sit down and the doc will be here in a minute."

Jace thought this would be a good time to introduce Luther to Hailey. He took her by the arm, and led her Luther was sitting, "Luther I would like for you to meet Hailey. And this is Steve."

She said, "Hello Steve." And turned to Luther "You have been hurt." He said "Steve is hurt worse than me." but she went to the back room and brought a wet cloth and washed Luther's face where dried blood has formed. He said "This is so nice of you Mam."

She said "Please call me Hailey."

"Just call me Luther Ma'am…I mean, Miss Hailey."

Jace looked at Steve and smiled, "I guess his wounds are worse than yours."

Steve smiled, "I guess so she seams to like working on him. That's Okay, if a pretty girl looked at me like that I would be all right too."

They laughed and Hailey turned red. Luther told them, "You leave miss Hailey alone she is doing a good job."

Jace said, "Sure looks like it."

Jennifer came running into the office and jumped into Jace's arms and said "I was so worried. I heard the shots and I didn't know what happened. I thought maybe you were hurt or worse. I had to see for myself." She kissed him and said "I am so glad this is over."

He said, "Me to but there may be more. I don't think McMurtry is going to give up that easy."

She held him close, "I don't want anything to happen to you."

"You just stay safe and I will be all right."

"I have to get ready just in case they try something else," Ben replied.

They all spoke at once, "if you need help just let us know. "

"Thanks I 'll probably call on you. I think I am going to need all the help I can get. With friends like you everything will be all right"

"Miss Hailey, would you like to go get something to eat?" Luther asked.

"I would but I am not off for lunch for another half hour."

Fred replied, "You go on and take as long as you like I will be here for a while. We need to take care of these boys. They are sure doing a job of taking care of this town."

They started out the door and Hank said, "Be careful when he starts eating he is dangerous."

They all laughed and Luther laughed, "I'm going to have to take care of you all when I get back." He smiled when they walked out the door.

Hailey said, "I don't like for them to talk about you like that."

Luther just smiled and said, "If they didn't like me they wouldn't kid me like that."

"Well I guess that is right but I don't like for people to put you down," she told him.

"I've been put down for years but these are the best friends I ever had."

Hailey thought for a bit, "I am glad you have such good friends. I think that Jace is a very good man and I think Jennifer thinks so too,"

"I know he thinks a lot of her. He is always thinking about her."

Jennifer said, "Jace why don't you and Ray come to the house and have lunch with Jessica, daddy and myself?" They said "Ok that would be fine."

Tim smiled, "I guess we're on our own men." Hank laughed and said, "Steve come and join us for lunch."

"I would like that," Steve answered.

After lunch Ben met everyone at the jail to get set up in case of another attempt on a jailbreak.

Hank and Bart were in their cell when they heard something at the cell window. Bart stood on the bunk and saw two men trying to get their attention. He said, "What do you want?"

"We are going to break you out at daybreak in the morning so be ready. "

Hank whispered, "What is going on."

"Some men are going to break us out in the morning." Hank told him.

"Tell them they better watch McCord and that big idiot because they are bad news for anyone that tried to break us out before,"Bart sneered.

He told them and they answered, "Don't worry because that early in the morning everyone will be asleep."

Bart said, "I hope so."

Jace and Ray sat on the porch with Jessica and Jennifer. They talked and laughed until late and Jace said "We better get some sleep because we may have a big day tomorrow. He kissed Jennifer and said good night and Ray held Jessica's hand. He said,"Goodnight"

She reached up and kissed him on the cheek, "You be careful tomorrow."

"I will," He told her. "I want to see you again and if I get hurt bad I wont be able to."

Jace and Ray walked down the street toward the hotel. Jace looked him in the eye, "Ray I want to tell you something and I don't want you to get mad at me."

Ray shifted himself. Very nervous, "I wont and if it is about Miss Jessica don't worry I really like her. I know I don't deserve her but I really like her."

"I am glad because I would not want her to get hurt," Jace told him.

Ray looked at him, "I wont hurt her and I won't let anyone else either. I wouldn't like to have you mad at me. You are the best friend I ever had."

He told him, "Good night Ray see you in the morning." They went to their rooms and tried to get some sleep. Jace lay awake thinking about all that had gone on and thought some thing was wrong. He finally let sleep come to him. He woke with a start and sat up and reached for his gun. He didn't hear anything but something had woke him and he didn't know what. He got up and walked to the window and looked out. Nothing was moving but something was wrong. He felt it so strong that he woke the rest of his friends and told them something was wrong but he couldn't tell what it was.

Hank said, "I feel something too. What do you think we should do?"

"Get ready and lets surround the jail out of sight and see what happens. "Jace told them. They each took a place and watched. It was starting to get daylight and the feeling was stronger that something was wrong. After about a half hour he thought he saw something move down the street. He looked into the night and tried to see what it was. All of a sudden he saw four men leading six horses. He knew that they were going to hit the jail. He tried to see the rest of his friends but everyone was well hid. He hoped they were alert and saw the men coming down the street. They reached the jail and two of the men went to the sheriff's office and went in and in a few minuets they came out with the two prisoners.

Jace said, "That's far enough boys we have you surrounded. Give up before its to late."

A shot went just over his head and he shot the man that had shot at him. After that everyone was shooting. He saw another one go down and then another one. He saw one get on his horse and lay low on the side of the horse like the Indians do. He got away and Hank and Bart yelled "We give up don't shoot."

Bart had been hit in the shoulder. Ben came up and had been hit in the leg and a flesh wound in his side.

Jace said, "Someone go get the doc."

They took everyone in the sheriff's office and the deputy on duty was out cold on the floor. They put him on the cot in the corner and put a cold towel on his head. The doc arrived and Ben said, "We have some business for you."

"I need to look at the deputy and make sure he don't have a concussion." the doc replied. He checked him and said "He will be alright. He will have a head ache for a day or two," He looked at Ben and patched his wounds.

"What about me I been hit too." Bart yelled.

The doc looked his way. "I should leave you that way but I'll take care of you. That is what I swore to do when I took the oath."

Fred came up then and asked "What's going on?"

"They tried a jailbreak and if Jace hadn't been so alert they would have gotten away with it." Ben replied.

Jennifer and Jessica came running up and went to Jace and Ray and said. "We were afraid you may have been hurt."

Fred pointed toward the girls. "I told you girls to stay there until I checked things out."

"We couldn't stand to wait here any longer. We were so worried." They told him.

Jessica kissed Ray and held him close. "I am all right and I would go through that again to get a kiss like that."

She just looked at him and held him. Jennifer spoke. "You all come to the house and Jessica and I will fix breakfast for you."

"You girls go on and start breakfast and we will be there in a little while. We have to wrap this up and then we will be there." Fred told them.

Jessica said. "Ok daddy but don't wait to long. We will have everything ready soon."

Just then Hailey came up. "Luther are you all right?"

"I sure am don't worry about me." He told her."

She said. "I can't help it I heard the shots and I just knew you were involved in it."

"I wonder who else will show up." Fred replied.

They laughed and Fred nodded toward her. "Hailey go home and get dressed and come to the house. Jennifer and Jessica are cooking breakfast."

"I will change and help them." She answered him.

They all met at Fred's house to eat and found all three girls busy making breakfast They sat down and Fred said, "Lets offer thanks for the day and no one was hurt." After thanks they all started eating. Jace noticed that Jennifer was with him and Jessica was with Ray and Hailey was with Luther. They ate and laughed and had a good morning.

Jennifer and Jessica told them, "Why don't you all go sit on the front porch and we will clean the kitchen and join you." They all sat on the porch and talked. Hank said, "Do you think they will try anything else?" Fred said, "I am afraid so only this time I fear what they might do."

"They tried early this morning so they may try again at night. Maybe I should make a trip to the Dakotas and see this man and get this taken care of," Jace said.

Fred looked worried, "I don't want you to do that because he has an army of men around him and you would get killed. I think if we just wait and the judge will be here next week and then it will be over."

"I could wire the U. S. Marshals office for help," Ben suggested.

Jace said, "I think we can handle this but we are going to have to be on alert all the time till the judge gets here."

"I have some business to take care of so I will see you later," Fred told them. Hank, Tim and Rick said they had to go too. The girls came out and sat with Jace, Ray and Luther.

Jennifer said, "I am so worried about you all I hope this will end soon." "The judge will be here next week and it will be over then," Jace told her Hoping to make everyone feel better. Jennifer answered, "I hope so we don't want anything to happen to any of you. I have looked all my life to find you and I don't want to loose you and I am sure Jessica and Hailey think the same thing."

"We do so please be careful" Jessica smiled. They talked for a while and decided they needed to check around town to be sure nothing was going on. They went to the sheriff's office and the deputy said, "The sheriff was down the street checking on a fight at the saloon."

Jace said, "I'll go check on him."

"I'll go with you," Luther told him. When they got to the saloon they found Ben and he had two men taking them outside to the jail. He asked, "Luther would you please take these two men to jail for me? Tell the deputy I will be there as soon as I can."

"Jace would you go with me I need to talk to you," Ben asked him.

They left and went to the telegraph office and he sent a wire. When he finished that he asked, " would you like to get a cup of coffee?"

Jace said, "Sure." and they went to the café and ordered.

"While I was in the saloon I heard one of the men I arrested say something about McMurtry and his plan. I didn't get it all but something is going on and we need to be careful. He is powerful and sneaky. I wouldn't put anything past him and what he might do."

"Well we will keep four or five at the jail and the rest will be checking around town. We can handle it if we use our heads and don't panic. We have some good men with us and we will take care of what ever he has planed. We are as smart as he is so we will outsmart him," Jace said.

"I hope you are right," Ben answered "I don't know what I would do with out you and the friends of yours. I'll make sure the town pays you all deputies pay. If it is a few days before he does anything we need to be careful and not get careless."

Jace said, "You're right so we'll talk about it to everyone every day so we stay alert."

"You sure have some good boys with you and I am glad they are staying here. We need good people here and I think three girls are really happy you all are here." Ben replied with a smile.

Jace smiled and said, "I know I am so happy I met Jennifer and I think she is a very special girl."

Ben told him, "She is I have known her since she was a small girl and her and her family are good people and I am happy you met them and brought good people with you."

When they got back to the jail they found the two men locked up and the deputy said, "Luther said hold them and you would be here soon."

"You did good and we will hold them until morning and let them sober up and release them," Ben said.

"Jace do you think it would do any good to question them?" Ben asked.

"I don,t think so but we could try."

Luther said "let me talk to them I will find out what they are hiding."

Jace said "No I think they are more afraid of McMurtry than they are of us."

"You may be right," Ben said " But I am still worried. I don't like not knowing what is going on. If I know what is going to happen I can handle it Ok. Bring the taller one out here and I will talk to him" The deputy brought him out and they sat in a chair and ben ask him, "What was McMurtry. Planning?"

He said "I don't know what is going on I was just standing there when the sheriff came in and started hitting me and dragged me here. I wasn't doing anything wrong,"

Jace said "I'll tell you one time if I find out your lying and anyone gets hurt because you lied I will come after you and you will not like it I promise you that." They decided that there was a waste of time talking to them.

Jace said, "I am ready to find something to eat."

"I'll stay here till you get back and then you can take over while I eat," Ben told them, "Tim and I will stay with the sheriff and the deputy Luther replied, "We'll be back soon as we can get a bite to eat. Jace told them. They went to the café and ordered and Ray said, "Do you think they will do anything today?"

"I don't know but we have to be ready just in case," Jace answered him. Hank asked, "What do you think they will do?" "I don't know" Jace replied "But he must be pretty mad and worried right now. He has tried and lost every time and I think he is getting desperate right about now. We will have to be ready day and night so I think the best thing is to sleep in the storeroom next to the jail. That way if anything happens we will be ready."

When they got back to relieve the others he told Ben what he thought and he said, "That's a good idea. We will all be ready all the time. I will have some bunks brought over for us to sleep on and we can fix a stove in there and eat there."

The sheriff and Luther and Tim left to eat and Jennifer and Jessica came to the sheriffs office. She ran and threw her arms around Jace and Jennifer did the same to Ray. He held her close and said "Honey I am afraid something is close to happening and I think he is going to go all out this time so I want you girls to stay home and don't go out unless you have to and then be very careful. Tell your dad I think Hailey should stay with you so she would not be so close to the jail."

She said, I will tell him and I know he will agree. I think I will get my friend Kimberly to stay with us and we can help each other."

He said, "Just stay safe I could not stand it if anything happened to you."

"I worry about you too."

"I can take care of myself if I don't have to worry about you. We are going to fix a place next door to sleep and eat so we will be close all the time," Jace told her.

"We could bring your food to you" She replied.

"No," He said "I don't want you anywhere near this jail. If you all stay home and don't go out till this is over I will feel better."

She said they would stay in the house and not go out unless it was something they had to do.

"Go get enough food to last and bring enough water and you should be safe till this is over." They kissed the girls and said, "We will see you in a few days." They went home and Jennifer went by Fred's office and told him what Jace said.

"That is a good idea," Fred said. "I want my girls safe and out of harms way They went to Kimberly's house and told her what they were doing and wanted her to spend the next few days with them. She said, "Let me ask my father he will be home in just a few minuets."

"We will wait and see what he says."

He came home a little later, "Hi girls what is going on. I ain't seen this many pretty girls together ever."

They laughed and told him what was going on and they wanted Kimberly and Hailey to stay the next few days with them. He said, "I heard about the men trying to break some men out of jail but I didn't know it was this bad."

"They had been trying to stop Jace since he left to go get them," Jennifer answered him.

"This Jace feller I hear he is a good man with a gun."

Jennifer said, "He is the best in the world."

Jerry Dawson smiled, "It sounds like you kind of like him?"

"I do Mr. Dawson," She replied.

He asked, "How does your father feel about this?"

"He likes Jace real good and is happy that he and I are dating."

"Oh so you are dating. Well if Fred is happy about it I guess I is alright then. I guess it is alright for Kim to go with you till the danger is over but you girls be very careful."

They told him bye and they would be careful.

They left and stopped at Hailey's house to pick up her clothes and talk to her father.

They went in her home and met Larry Murphy and he said, "Hi girls how are all you pretty girls doing together today?"

Jennifer spoke, "Mr Murphy we are going to our house and stay until the trouble at the jail is over."

"I heard there was an attempted jail break. Is everything ok there?" He ask.

"Well we don't know but the men at the jail are going to guard it day and night until the trouble is over," Jessica replied.

"Well you girls be careful and if you need anything call me. Watch out for Hailey. I worry about my daughter. Don't get me wrong I worry about all of you," Larry said.

"We will watch out for her and see that she is safe,"Jennifer answered

"Well I hear this Jace McCord is very good with a gun?" He replied.

Jennifer said, "Yes sir he is very good."

Larry Murphy said, "Sounds like you like him pretty good. How does your father like that?"

"He likes Jace real good and is happy about it. You should ask your daughter about Luther."

"Jennifer," Hailey said

:Well what is this about this Luther, Hailey?" He asked her.

"He is a very wonderful man and so brave. He is very big and good looking but I will tell you all about him when I get back home.

"Well it sounds like you better tell me more about him, but right now I think you better take Mr Lawson's advice and stay with Jessica and Jennifer until this is over. I'll check on you girls every day and make sure you are all Ok."

Jennifer kissed him on the cheek, "Thank you Mr. Murphy." They went upstairs and got Hailey's things. They went home and the girls fixed everything so they could sleep in the same room.

Kimberly said, "This is going to be fun."

"It would be if we didn't worry about the men at the jail," Jennifer told them.

Jessica smiled, "I think you are worried more about Jace than all of the rest of them."

" I think you are worried more about Ray than anyone else too" Jennifer replied. "I really love Jace and I want to spend the rest of my life with him and I pray nothing happens to any of them."

Hailey said, "Sounds serious."

"I really worry about Ray too,"Jessica told them..

Hailey told them, "I am worried about Luther too. I really like him and I don't want to loose him."

Kim asked, "What is going on here?"

Hailey explained, "These men came back with Jace. We found we really liked some of them better than others."

She said,"Oh which one do you like?"

"have you seen the really big man with them?"

"Yes he is quite a big man. I'll bet if anyone hurt you they would be in big trouble," Kimberly said.

"I think he is and he is not only big and strong but he is the most gentle person I ever met. He held my hand and I thought how he could crush it so easy but he was so careful and held me like I might break. I never felt so safe in my life as when I am with him."

Jessica said, "You need to meet them they are the greatest men you ever met and I mean all of them. You might find one you like."

"I don't think so I haven't found anyone I care about around here." Kimberly told them.

They talked and laughed the rest of the day and were going to stay in the house safe so the men wouldn't be worried about them. Her father could keep her informed as to what was going on.

Jace thought about taking one of the two that the sheriff brought in an beating a confession out of him but that would make him as bad as they were. He wanted to know what they were planning. He was having trouble sleeping and he would be glad when it was over. He thought about Jessica and her family and wanted this to be over so they could get their lives on the right track. He still worried about Jennifer and how they could be happy if he always had to look behind him the rest of his life. He knew he really loved her. He loved Karen but not this way or this much. Jennifer was something very special and he didn't want anything to happen to her like it did Karen and their baby girl. It was his turn to stay at the jail with Ray and Rick. They would have a long night but they had to do it till the judge came and had the trial. He knew their father was getting more determined to get them out but what would he try. He had tried everything else and failed so what was next. He would not give up and after the trial if they were found guilty and hanged what then. Would McMurtry take revenge out on the town? He thought I have to stop thinking about this or I will go crazy. He had been able to take anything after the war but now he had

Jennifer to think about and he liked thinking about her. Everything will work out he thought to himself.

Ray and Rick walked in and said, "We are ready to take care of anything that comes our way."

"Good I just hope nothing comes our way too bad," Jace replied as he wondered what time it was and ask if one of them had a watch.

Rick said, "It is ten after two."

Jace asked, "How long can a night be. It fells like we have been here a long time."

"Rest a while and I will keep watch," Ray told him.

Jace answered, "No I think we better all be alert and ready."

"I will be happy when we can get this over I think I have found everything I have ever wanted," Ray told him.

Jace said, "I have to but we have to not think about that until this is over. If you think about things like that if makes you afraid to die and you get weak. Just think how we have to face anyone coming here and don't let up for anything. If you fight with all you have and don't give up we will come out ahead. No matter what happens don't stop until it is over and you will win

"I guess you are right. I think Rick and Tim and me gave up in phoenix and that is why were beaten. You came along and took on all the things we feared. We will be with you no matter what," Ray told him.

"I know you will," Jace said "You are good men and I am happy to fight alongside you."

They sat and didn't talk for a while when Rick spoke, "look the sun is starting to come up. I am so glad this night is over."

"I am hungry and could eat a whole cow." Ray said.

"Now you sound like Luther," Rick smiled. "I will go hunt one up for you."

Ben came in, "I'll eat breakfast and then come to relieve you."

They waited till Ben and the rest of his friends came to relieve them and started to leave when Ben said, "The café brought food for them so they don't have to cook."

"Good," Rick replied. "I never was a good cook anyway."

They ate and came back to the jail. He told Ben that they had a good night with no problems. Just then Steve Axton came in, "Sheriff if you need some more help I will be glad to help you."

"Thanks but right now we are all right but if we need you I will call you."

All of a sudden Fred came in to the sheriffs office and had blood running down his face. He said, "Jace they took Jennifer."

"Who took her?" Jace asked. The look in his eyes was cold and mean.

"I don't know they just came in and took her."

He told Luther to get a wet rag to wash his face. He took the rag and washed the blood off, "Where is Jennifer and who took her?"

Fred look at him, "Four men broke in and took Jennifer and said when we let the prisoners go they would let her go."

"They wont let her go even if we did let them go. Rick would you get me some supplies while I saddle my horse," Jace told him.

Luther, Ray, Tim and Hank spoke up, "We are going with you."

"You better hurry because I am leaving soon as I can. I am not going to play with these men I am going to kill them or die myself, so be sure you want to go."

They told him they were sure.

Steve Axton said, "I want to come to."

Jace told him, "I appreciate you wanting to help but I would feel better if you stayed here in case some of them come back."

He wasn't happy but he agreed to stay and guard the town.

He said "Fred which way did they go?"

"They left and rode north. I watched as long as I could to make sure. They broke in and I ran for my gun on the wall and one of them hit me with his pistol," Fred told him.

"Don't worry I will get her back," Jace replied

"Steve can you help me now?." Ben asked him.

"Sure what ever you need."

Jace met them back at the jail when they all had their horses saddled and ready.

Rick said, "I want to go with you."

"I need you to stay here and help Ben and Steve just in case they come back."

"Ok what ever you say. Tim is a good tracker, he lived with the Indians for a couple of years and knows a lot of their ways."

"Good I can use all the help I can get," Jace said "Ben watch out this could be a trick to get us out of town."

"I'll be careful just get Jennifer back safe." Ben told him "Plus I have two good men to help me."

They mounted up and left headed north trying to pick up the trail.

Tim held his hand up, "Wait and let me find the trail." He rode ahead and got off his horse and looked around. He called and said, "I found it come on." They left and followed Tim as he found the trail. Sometimes it was slow and sometimes they could move pretty fast.

"They aren't trying to cover their trail."

Jace said, "They must know we will follow so they are going to try to ambush us. looks like they are headed north so I will take Hank with me and try to circle around and get ahead of them and stop any ambush attempt."

"Good idea," Tim told him.

"Watch your self because if we fail or they set up the ambush sooner than we can get ahead of them you might get caught in the ambush your selves," Jace told them

They said they would be careful. Jace and Hank left and rode hard for a while and let up so the horses would not tire to quick. They made good time and Jace said, "I know a place where they could set up a good ambush."

They rode past the place Jace told him about and had to climb some places that the horses had a hard time getting up but they made it and circled around and when they were close Jace said, "Lets leave the horses here and walk. If they are there we can sneak up on them."

They walked for a while when Jace told him, "Get down and lets crawl up this next hill. I think they will be just over the next rise if they are planning an attempt to stop us."

They crawled to the top and Jace took off his hat and eased up to look over the top. Sure enough there were three men waiting with rifles. He waived at Hank and he saw them, "Go around the other side of that big rock and get ready. I am going to give them a chance to give up but if they start shooting then we'll get them all."

He eased around the rock and waited till he heard Jace say, "You men give up we have you surrounded."

They started shooting and Hank and Jace opened up and shot all three of them. He ran down and found one of them still breathing. He asked him, "Where are they taking the girl?"

He coughed and said "I ain't going to tell you."

"I will get help for you if you tell me."

"I am a goner any how I can't last much longer so you better let them boys in jail go or you will never see the girl again."

Jace pulled his six-gun and put it to his head and Hank stopped him, "Jace he is gone don't waste a bullet."

They saw Luther, Ray and Tim coming and waived to them.

They saw them and rode to the bottom of the hill. Tim asked, "Did you find them?"

"We found three of 'em. They were more of 'em than Fred knew about. I think they have four or five with 'em now and these were left here just in case they were chased out of town. Let us get out horses and we will meet you down the trail a ways," Jace said

They left and Jace and Hank reached their horses and met the other three down the trail and Tim told everyone, "They are still going the same way."

"I think they are headed someplace and they will not turn till they get there," Jace replied.

They rode till dark and Tim said, "I can't see the trail we need to stop for the night."

"You stop I am going to get Jennifer back," Jace answered.

Luther said "Jace don't do this we will get her back but we have to use our heads like you always told us to do."

He sat down and put his head on his knees and sat there for a while. Hank sat beside him and said, "I know how you feel but we have to take out time to think and not just run wild without a plan."

"I know you are right I just don't think I could stand it if anything happens to Jennifer."

Hank put his hand on his shoulder, "They are not going to hurt her till they get the prisoners out because they are afraid of McMurtry."

"I am not afraid of him and when we get Jennifer home safe I am going to take care of this once and for all."

"We're with you. We will get him what ever it takes," Luther told him

"Thanks men I am sorry I lost my head."

"I know how I would feel if it were Jessica and I like Jennifer too so we will get her back safe and take her home. Then we will take care of McMurtry," Ray told him.

They had a cold camp just in case they were close enough for the men they were chasing to see the fire. They ate jerky and drank water.

Luther broke the silence. "I will be glad when this is over I can't live on this stuff."

They all smiled and Jace grinned, "Thanks Luther you make me feel like we are going to do good and get her back."

They fixed the camp and lay down to sleep. Jace could not sleep and he thought of Jennifer out there afraid and alone. He would get her back and the ones responsible for this would pay with their lives. No one was going to hurt her and get away with it.

Jace woke an the sun was just starting to come up. The sky was beginning to show a little light and he thought they could get started. He saddled his horse and the rest of them were beginning to wake up. They saddled and were ready to go soon after he was.

"I think I can pick up the trail now," Tim decided.

They started out and was going north still. They found where they camped last night and Jace found where they had tied Jennifer to a tree. He was so mad he wanted to catch them as soon as he could and make them pay.

Tim guessed, "They are about three or four hours ahead of us. I think if we ride hard maybe we can catch them by tonight."

Jace said, "let's ride I want to catch them as soon as possible. I don't want her to have to spend any more. time with that scum than she has to."

"What are we going to do when we catch them?" Hank asked. "Jennifer will be in danger because if she is not hit by a stray bullet they will try to shoot her."

Jace shook his head, "I don't know but when we catch them I will do something to get her away from them. We will have to see what it looks like when we get there."

They rode hard the rest of the day and made good time. Tim told them, "The tracks are fresh and they're not very far ahead."

"I hope we're close because our horses are not going to last long like we have been riding them," Ray said.

It was starting to get dark and Jace looked at them, "I am not going to stop tonight till I get her back."

"It won't do any good if you get killed. That wont help her any so we need to use our heads," Hank replied.

"Look" Luther pointed, "I think I see a light up ahead."

Jace was excited, "It looks like a campfire."

They stopped and. got off the horses. Jace walked as close as he could and then got down on his belly and crawled till he could see them. He could see three men but could not find Jennifer. He crawled closer and all of a sudden he was close to a man in the woods. He didn't expect a guard but now he was in trouble. He didn't move or hardly breathe. His heart was about to explode. He thought he would pass out for a while. He hoped none of the rest of them would try to follow him because they might run into one of the guards. He waited till the man said, "I am coming in someone else can stand out here. I want something to eat and drink."

One of the men in the camp yelled, "Come on in Pete can take your place."

"Why do I have to take his place. Ted ain't had a turn watching and I have."

The leader or the one giving all the orders said, "Shut up and get out there before I shoot you. I am tired of listening to you all cry every time you have to stand watch."

"Now listen we only have to take her to Julesburg and hold

her till he gets his boys out of jail then we can do what ever we want."

One of the other men grinned real big, "I want her first."

The leader spoke, "I get her first and the rest of you can fight over what is left."

Jace was so mad he put his sights on the leader and wanted to pull the trigger but he knew it would put Jennifer in danger so he crawled back to where the rest of his men were and told them what he heard.

Hank asked, "How are we going to get her out?"

"The rest of you keep the guards busy and I am going in there and get her."

Hanks told him "Don't do that because you will get killed."

"If I do tell Jennifer I love her and want her to be safe."

Hank started to tell him, "Lets get a plan and we can get her out."

"Don't try to stop me I am going to get her and I am going to do it now."

He left running toward the camp and someone in the camp yelled, "Someone's coming."

The leader said, "Get ready it may be the boys we left to ambush them."

Jace ran to the side where Jennifer was tied and started shooting. He got two of them before they started shooting back. He felt a sting in his leg but he shot one more of them in the chest. Another one shot him in the arm and he got him between the eyes. He heard the rest of his bunch shooting around him. He ran to Jennifer and took her gag out and untied her. She fell in his arms and started crying. He held her close and told her "Everything will be all right now."

She held him, "I knew you would come after me."

She was more worried about him than she was herself. He

helped her up and the rest of his men came in and patted her on the arm and said we are so glad you are all right.

She hugged all of them, "How could I not be all right with friends like you."

She held on to Jace, "I feel so safe in your arms."

He jerked back and she asked, "What's wrong?" and then she saw the blood on his shirt and then on his leg.

"Come here and let me take care of you I didn't realize you were hurt. You are like a mad man when you came in here. I just knew you weren't going to get out of here. I was so afraid. I don't want anything to happen to you. I love you and I want you to always be with me."

He held onto her, "don't worry just stay safe and I can take care of myself."

Ray came over and sat down where they were, "Is Jessica Okay?"

"Yes," She replied. "They just wanted me to hold for ransom till you let the men in jail out. How is daddy? he was hurt?"

"He is Okay just a crease on his head where one of them hit him," Jace answered.

Luther said, "Jace two of these men are still alive. What so you want to do with them?"

"If they can make it back we will take them with us if not we will leave them here for the buzzards."

Luther took the two men and tied them to a tree and. The one called Pete said, "I am hurt you are supposed to take care of me."

Luther grabbed his arm, "Just be glad you didn't hurt any of the girls, and one called Hailey you better not have hurt, or you wont make it to the trial. Now sit there and shut up before you make me mad."

Ted said, "Mr. McMurtry will take care of you all and we will get free."

Jace came over, "Thanks for telling me for sure who is behind all this. I thought it was him but now I know for sure."

"You can't prove anything, and the law can't touch him."

"I am not talking about the law," Jace told him "I'll take care of him myself."

"You better leave him alone he has a lot of men and he'll kill you and we'll be free."

Well Jace said, "He may get me but not before I get him. Now shut up or I will let Luther have you for something to beat around."

They looked at Luther and thought it was a good idea to keep quiet.

The next morning Jace woke and Jennifer was on his arm close to him with a smile on her face. He started to get up without waking her. She spoke to him, "Don't go, I have never felt so good in my life. I like being here with you."

"On this old hard ground?" He asked.

"I would rather be here with you than anywhere else. I don't like being without you and I heard what you told that man last night about taking care of that man that is causing all our trouble. Please don't go because I may never see you again."

"Don't worry about that now lets just get you home safe and let your family know you are alright."

"Ok," she replied and they packed up and had a good breakfast and started out.

Jace said, "We better keep our eyes open because he might try something before we get home." They rode steady that day and made good time.

"Will we make it home tomorrow?" Luther asked.

"I don't think so. Why are you in such a hurry to get home could it be that pretty little girl there?" Jace smiled.

"Well yes I never saw anyone as pretty as her and surly not

one that liked me. She said I was a gentle man. I been called lots of things but never that."

Jace and the rest of them laughed, "Good for you Luther. We are glad you met her and like her because she sure likes you."

"I don't know about that but I sure like her."

Jennifer answered, "Luther she does like you and you are a gentle man when you are with women. With men I don't know of anyone that could match you."

They stopped along a creek and had dinner. They rested for a while so Jennifer could rest before they started again. She said, "You are the greatest men I ever met besides my father."

Hank sat by her, "Miss Jennifer I never knew anyone like you and your family. I don't have a family and I never felt toward anyone like I do the people I met here. Jace there has become a very good friend and I am happy to know people like you and you friends and family."

"You don't have a girl friend or anything?"

"No." He replied. "If I ever met anyone like you I would sure try to get her to like me."

"I want you to meet my friend Kimberly when we get home. I think you will like her and I think she will like you. You don't have to get someone to like you. They like you or not. I think Kim will like you."

"I don't know how she could like me. I am not someone girls seem to go for," He answered..

"I like you and I am a girl. You are a loyal friend and you risk your life to save me. That shows good character. I think you are a good man and Jace likes you and that says a lot to me."

Jace told them, "We better get going so we can make as much time as we can today.

They stopped at sundown and made camp for the night. They took what supplies the outlaws had and guns and ammunition they found. They turned most of the horses loose except the ones they needed for packhorses. They ate a good meal and got ready to sleep. Jace made Jennifer a place to sleep and took his things over a little ways.

She said, "No I want you here with me."

"It wouldn't be right for me to lay with you like that," Jace told her.

"It wouldn't be right to leave me alone after what I have been through."

The rest of his friends said, "She's right you know."

"Okay, but I don't know how I feel about having you so close."

She said, "Just hold me and we can go to sleep."

He could feel her warm breath on his neck and he thought I have never been so happy and contented in my life. He thought about the future and how it would be with her. He suddenly thought what he had ahead of him and he knew there was no way he could be happy and be with her until he took care of the man that had been trying to kill him since he left for Yuma. He had almost killed Fred and Jennifer and did kill some of his friends. He would have to take care of this before he could plan any kind of life with her. He finally drifted off to sleep and woke sometime in the night. He looked at Jennifer there in his arms. He watched her sleep and thought how did I get such a beautiful girl? Just as the sun was starting to color the sky he woke up. He moved his arm from under her head and got up with out waking her. He started a fire and put on some coffee. The rest of the group woke at the smell of fresh coffee brewing. Jennifer came over and put her hand on his shoulder.

"I never felt so safe and comfortable in my life."

He told her, "I slept pretty good too. It was hard to sleep with you so close."

Hank said, "Will we get back to town today?"

They packed up and started toward home and rode till the afternoon.

A young boy came to Ben and said, "Sheriff I think miss Jennifer and the men that went after her is coming up the road toward town."

Ben ran out and met them half way to town.

Fred came out with a bandage on his head and ran down the road to meet them. Jennifer jumped off her horse and ran to him. He held her and said, "I was so afraid I might never see you again."

"As long as Jace is around I feel like I will be all right."

He went to Jace as he was getting off his horse, "How can I ever thank you. This is two times you have saved her."

"Don't worry I can't let anything happen to her. I would be lost without her," He told him.

"I need to talk to you and Ben and all my friends as soon as we get cleaned up and get Jennifer home safe."

Just then Jessica, Hailey and Kimberly came running up the road calling Jennifer. They all ran up and put their arms around her and said they were so happy to see her.

Kimberly said, "Is this Mr. McCord ?"

Jennifer told her, "This is Jace and Jace this is my friend Kimberly."

Jace took off his hat and said, "Glad to meet you Ma'am.

"I have heard so much about you and I am glad to finally meet you. You are all Jennifer talks about."

Jennifer said, "Kim I want you to meet Hank Lassiter."

"Hello Mr. Lassiter," She replied."

"Hi Miss Kimberly glad to meet you."

Fred said, "Why don't you all go get cleaned up and meet us at the hotel café and I will treat you all to dinner."

Luther grinned real big, "Sounds good to me." Hailey had his hand in hers and looking at him, she was in another world.

Jessica was holding Ray and said I was so afraid for you and hoped you would come home to me. You all took such a great risk."

"We had to get Jennifer home safe. She is such a great lady. All the boys think she if wonderful but we don't want to make Jace mad," Ray smiled.

"I know and I don't know how to thank you all for that."

Luther said, "Sheriff if you could put these two men in jail I would feel better."

Ben told his deputy "Put them in a cell and we will take care of them later."

One of the men groaned, "I'm hurt."

Ben said, "Well so are some of our men and they will be taken care of first."

It was the first time Ben noticed Jace had been wounded. He said, "lets get him to the doctor and get him taken care of."

"Ray has been wounded too" Jessica told them.

"It's just a scratch," He told them.

"Well it's bleeding," She answered.

Fred said, "lets get the doc and get everyone checked out."

After they left the doctors office Ben said, "The doc was going to check the two in jail. He said he wouldn't be to careful about tending their wounds."

After everyone was cleaned up they met at the hotel café to eat. When Jace got there some of the rest of his bunch was there. They talked for a while and the waiter came out, "Mr. Lawson said I was to take care of you when you arrived. I have a table waiting for you."

They talked for a while and drank coffee. Ray jumped up and they didn't know what was going on. Jace had his gun in his hand and was ready for what ever was going on. He noticed the smile on Rays face and looked around and saw Fred and the girls coming in. Fred said, "You are the fastest man I ever saw. You had that gun in your hand before I knew you were even going for it."

"Pays to be ready."

Jennifer jumped in his arms and kissed him, "I missed you."

"Jennifer you are in public," Fred said.

"I don't care daddy I love him and I don't care who knows it," Jennifer told him.

Jessica and Hailey went to Ray and Luther and put their arms around them. Luther turned red and everyone laughed. He said, "I ain't used to someone really liking me just for me. I think people like me because I am big and they are scared of me, but this pretty little girl likes me just because and I can't believe it."

She said, "You better believe it because I like you because you are so big but you are really gentle and you make me feel so safe."

They sat down and ordered their meal and ate while they talked.

Fred spoke, "I would like to thank you all for saving my daughters life. I was afraid I would never see her again.

Ray told him, "We really didn't do much.You should have seen Jace, he ran in their camp yelling and shooting. I was afraid and I was on his side,

Luther said, "I ain't been afraid of any man before but I was afraid of Jace when he went in there yelling and hollering. I never seen nothing like it in my life."

Fred asked, "Weren't you afraid that Jennifer would get hit?"

"No," He told him "I saw her tied to a tree and I came in so when they were shooting at me they would forget about her and she was out of the line of fire."

Ben said, "What are we going to do about the men in jail? We know McMurtry will try to get them out again."

"I am going to see him and tell him to leave us alone," Jace replied.

Ben said, "That won't do any good he does what ever he wants to do and no one tells him what to do."

Jace smiled, "No one ever ask like I am going to ask."

All the men at the table said we will go with you.

"We need to leave some here to watch the prisoners and help Ben.

Ben shook his head, "No I'll get a few deputies around town and take care of things here. You'll need all the men you can get to help you."

Luther said, "Steve Axton said he wanted to go with us when we went."

"Do you think we can trust him?" Jace asked.

"He is a good man he just got mixed up with the wrong people and is sorry for it now. He thinks no one will ever trust him again. He didn't know about the trouble we were having and when the men offered him money to back them up he didn't know what was going on but yea I think you could trust him at your back in a fight,"Luther answered.

"Good enough," Jace said "If you like him I think I can trust him."

Luther said, "I never had anyone trust me and take my word before. I think I have found what I have been looking for all my life."

"Well you have some good friends now. I would trust you to back me in a fight anytime. Jace told him.

After they ate Jace went to the sheriffs office and talked to Ben and Fred about the things that lay ahead. Jace asked, "How far is it to McMurtry's place?"

"I think it is about two hundred and fifty miles," Ben told him.

"We better get started then if it is that far. I need to get our horses and supplies ready to go. I will talk to the boys and see how many want to go with me. I don't want anyone getting hurt but I will need help if things are like every one says it is."

He met Luther and Ray at the hotel and ask if they wanted to go. They said, "yes"

"Where is Rick and Tim?" Jace asked.

Ray told him, "They were at the store to pick up some things."

"lets go meet them because we will need some things for the trail."

They met them at the store and he ask, " Are you boys interested in going with us?"

They said, "yes"

Just then Hank came in,"When do we leave?"

"I guess this means you heard and want to go."

"I talked to Ben just now and he told me. And yes I do want to go," Hank answered.

Just then Steve walked in, "I would like to go."

Fred came in, "Can I do anything to help."

Jace said, "Do you know anyplace we can put our supplies till we leave in the morning?"

"Sure you can put them in my storage building right next to the livery."

"That will be fine we will leave early in the morning."We may not see you before we leave so I will say goodbye now."

"Aren't you going to tell the girls that you are leaving?" Fred asked.

"I think it would be better if they didn't know till we were gone. They would worry too much."Jace told him.

Ben said, "They will worry just as much if you tell them or not I think you should tell them."

"Maybe you're right we will come by later when we finish here," Jace replied.

Fred said, "I will have all them at my house so you can see all four of them at once."

"Thanks," Jace smiled.

They met back at the hotel and talked about their trip. Steve said, "I'll sleep in the livery so I can be ready when you are."

"No," Jace told him. "You get a room here and we will make sure you are ready when we get started. We better go tell the girls."

Luther said, "I don't think I can tell Miss Hailey. She might get mad and I wouldn't like that."

"You know this is funny. You scare all men and one little girl has you afraid to tell her something. If we have to tell them you do too."

Ray laughed, "I didn't think you were afraid of anyone."

"I'm not afraid of any man but she is so pretty and so small. I couldn't do anything to hurt her and no one else better hurt her either."

They sat and talked for a while and Rick said, "What are you going to do when we get back?"

Jace answered, "I think I will go to New Mexico and check on my place. I would like to start raising cattle and horses again."

"Do you need any help?" Rick asked.

"I will and I was going to talk to you all when this is over. I have plans and I want to see what you all thought about them."

Tim asked, "What about Miss Jennifer?"

Jace said, "My plans include her if she is interested."

They laughed, "I think she is interested."

Ray chimed in, "I would like to see if Jessica would like that too. What about you Luther?"

"I can't ask Miss Hailey to follow me like that."

"Why not she likes you a lot."

He said, "I sure like her too. But I don't think she would be interested in going a long off with me."

"We will make plans when we get back and talk to the girls then.

We have a long way to go so I think we better get started. We can spend tomorrow-getting supplies and get the horses ready."

"What about the gunshot wounds you got getting Miss Jennifer back," Rick wondered.

"They are a little sore but I will be all right. I want to get this business over so we can make plans," Jace replied.

Rick asked, "Do you have any plans on what we are going to do when we get there?"

"I have a general plan but we will have to look things over when we get there. I need to talk to Ben and Fred so I will see you all later."

Jace went to the sheriff's office and ask where Ben was. The deputy said, "I think he went to the store said he would be back in a little while."

"Thanks," Jace replied an he went out the door toward Fred's office and saw Ben coming down the street. He waved, "You have a minute Ben?"

"Sure what do you need."

"I need to talk to you and Fred. Lets go by his office and see if he is there," Jace answered.

They opened the door and Hailey said, "Hi how is Luther?"

"He is fine is Fred in?"

"I will tell him you are here." She came out and said "He said tell you to come right in."

They went in and Fred said, "Sit down."

"I wanted to ask if either of you knew anything about McMurtry and his land or the lay out of the area or anything that will help on our trip to take care of this problem?"

"Well Jace I wish I did but I don't know much about the layout of his land. Maybe if you would wait and it will all be over soon and we can forget him and all this problem."

"Fred he just kidnaped your daughter. He's not going to stop. When those boys of his hang There is no telling what he might do. he is not going to forget or let this town forget. He will blame this town for his boy's death and take it out on all the people here."

"What can you do against so many?"

Jace said, "I don't know but I have stood before great odds before. I have a plan but I need to get the lay of the land when we get there."

Fred spoke, "Please don't take any chances if something happened to you Jennifer would never forgive me for letting you go."

He said, "I know but she would be in danger if I stay and do nothing and I don't want her in any danger ever again."

Ben and Fred told him all they knew about McMurtry and his ranch, which wasn't much, but it helped some. They ate and went to their rooms to get good nights sleep before they left. Jace started up the stairs when he heard Jennifer call his name. He turned and went to meet her. He took her in his arms and kissed her and held her close.

She said, "I am so worried about this trip. I wish you didn't have to go. We have grown to like all the friends you brought back with you and don't want anything to happen to you."

"Don't worry I will see you tomorrow and we can talk. We will be careful and try not to get hurt. We will only be gone a couple of weeks if everything goes Ok." He kissed her and said "Come on I will walk you home."

"I will be all right," She told him

"Till this over I want you girls to stay close to home."

"Do you expect more trouble?" She asked.

"I don't know," He told her. "But if we can get there soon enough maybe he won't have time to cause more trouble."

He walked her home and kissed her good night and said, "I will see you in the morning."

He felt his door and saw the toothpick he had placed there was still there. An old trick he learned from a friend of his. He lay down with his gun on the bedpost near his head so he could get at it if he needed it and lay down. So many things running through his head. Finally he drifted off to sleep. When he woke the sun was just starting to make a streak in the sky. He got up and washed his face and went down to breakfast. He met Hank and Tim there and Steve was just coming down the stairs. They went in and ordered breakfast when the rest of them came down. While they were eating Steve said, "Jace I want to let you know I never had anyone treat me like you boys do. Luther said you was good men but I've been a little gun shy if you know what I mean."

"You just live like you have since we met you and you will have us as your friends."

"I will, I am glad you trusted me and let me go with you on this trip. I promise I wont let you down."

"We were in Phoenix and Jace took us with him and we have had a great life since then. You stick with him and you will be Okay," Ray told him.

They finished breakfast and Jace said "Luther you and Steve go get the horses ready and we will leave in the morning. Rick and Ray if you will go to the store and get the supplies ready we will store them at Fred's warehouse by the livery till morning. Tim you and Hank come with me and we will meet back here this evening for supper."

They all took off and Jace and the men he took went to the sheriff's office and told Ben they needed some guns. He said, "I think I can help you. I have took a lot of guns over the years that never got claimed."

They met back at the hotel that evening and had their meal and Jace, Ray Hank and Luther went to Fred's house to see the girls. They sat on the porch and talked about the trip the men were going on. They all were afraid for them. Jace said, "When we get back I want to talk to all the men that came back with me and you girls and Fred. I have something I want to talk about and it concerns you all."

Jennifer asked, "What is it?"

"I will tell you when I get back. You want to go for a walk?"

She said, "Sure."

They walked down the street and talked. He took her hand and went to an old deserted building and took her in his arms and looked deep into the prettiest blue eyes he ever seen. He said, "You do know I love you don't you?"

"Yes," She replied " And you know how I feel about you don't you."

"Yes I do," He replied. "We will be back soon and I have some things I want to tell you."

"I am worried about you but I understand why you have to go," She told him.

"If I thought he would leave us alone I wouldn't go but he will blame this town for the death of his boys and he will want to punish us for that. We will be back soon and everything will be all right then."

He kissed her and said "I better get you home and get to sleep. We have a long day tomorrow."

They walked up the walk to her house and the girls and Luther and Ray were there. He said, "Where is Hank and Kimberly?"

"They went in the house she wanted to show him something she found about things that happened in the past."

They walked out just then and Jace said "I want you girls to stay together while we are gone because I don't know what they might try so be careful while we are gone."

They told the girls goodnight and were ready to leave. Hailey said, "Luther please be careful."

She pulled him down and kissed him. He turned red and said, "I will and you do like Jace said and be careful. I will be all right but I will worry about you."

They left and went back to their rooms. Jace told the night clerk to wake him at four in the morning.

Jace heard someone coming down the hall and he jumped up and grabbed his gun and stood behind the door. A knock on the door, "Mr. McCord it is four and you said wake you."

He opened the door and said, "Thanks" and gave him a coin from his pocket.

He finished dressing and woke the others, "I will meet you at the livery."

The man that ran the café said he would open early and have breakfast ready for them. He walked to the livery and sure enough the café was lite up and the man was in there cooking. He started getting the horses ready when the rest of his men showed up and helped load their supplies. After they were ready they went to the café and ate breakfast. He told the man, "Thanks for opening and feeding us."

He said, "What you have done for this town is thanks enough. If you had not been here those ole boys would have took the prisoners and killed half the men in town."

"I just wanted to keep the men in jail till they could stand trial."

"Be careful because that old man of theirs is a bad one and he will stop at nothing to get even. I don't think he even cares so much about his boys he just don't like having someone tell him no."

"He better get used to it because that is what we are headed up there to tell him," Jace nodded and they left.

They finished breakfast and met at the livery. They were saddled and the packhorses were ready. They started down the road and he saw Jennifer's house. He had never worried before but now he thought what if I don't come back. He shook that from his head and thought about what they were going to do. You think about what you have to live for and you may not make it. He knew they were going to have to get tough and put this above everything else. Hank rode up beside him and said, "What are we going to do when we get there?"

"I have a plan working but I haven't got the whole plan and till I do I think I better work it out before I tell you. I don't want to put things to you all till I have it worked out. We might get confused if we think about to many things at once."

They rode till they came to a large stream and Jace said, "Lets stop and water the horses and let them rest. We can eat and be on our way."

They rode till dark and made camp by a good creek. They hobbled the horses and made camp. While they were eating Jace said, "Luther you and Steve may come in handy for some of the things I am planning."

Steve answered, "What ever you want me and Luther can take care of it for you."

"I think so too. I haven't worked out all the plans yet but I am working on it and when I get everything worked out I will get with everyone and lay it out."

They woke early and ate and saddled the horses and had an early start. Luther said “Feels like it is getting colder.” Luther said.

“It is and will get colder the closer we get to the Dakotas.”

They rode all morning and hardly said anything. It was past noon when Hank said, “We need to rest the horses. “

”Good idea and we can eat while we are stopped.”

They hobbled the horses and let them graze while they ate. They were all getting on edge thinking about what they had facing them. Jace said, “Just don’t think about it and everything will be Ok. When we get there and start just don’t stop and back down. In a fight like this you have to give all you have and a little more. I have a plan I am working on and I don’t think we are going to have as much trouble as we think. If we get all worked up and let ourselves get thinking about things like the girls and how much we have to live for we will loose. For now just forget anything in the past and think about this trip and what we have to do. I think we will do all right but I can’t promise.”

They saddled the horses and started riding. They were not talking and Jace hoped they would be Ok in this fight. He knew how Hank and Luther would be in a fight but he had not been with the rest of them in a fight where they were tested in battle.

They had ridden for a few days when Jace said, “I think we are close to Mitchell South Dakota.”

Luther asked, “Is that were we are headed?”

“Yea, and we have to find his place. I hope we don’t have any trouble finding him.”

Hank said, “Let me and Luther go in ahead and act like a couple of cowhands needing a job.”

“Ok,” Jace replied “But be careful. We will ride in form the other side and if you have any trouble fire your gun twice and we will come on the run.”

"That is a good idea"

They split up and Jace and the rest of them went to the other end of town and rode in slow. He thought to go to the sheriff's office and see if he could find out anything. He got off his horse in front of the sheriffs office and told the others to wait for him. He went in and there was a deputy with his feet on the desk. He was very overweight and looked and smelled like he hadn't had a bath in a long time. He said "Yea can I help you?"

"I would like to talk to the sheriff." Jace told him"

He said, "Don't know where he is, but what do you want, I can help you."

"No, I want to talk to the sheriff."

The deputy got up and said, "Listen mister I don't like smart fellers like you coming in here and acting like you are better than me."

"I didn't say that, all I said I need to see the sheriff." He touched the butt of his pistol and the deputy backed up."

"I don't want any trouble mister."

"I don't want any trouble either," Jace told him. "But I won't stand here and let you give me a bad time."

He saw something in Jaces eyes that told him not to push any farther. Jace turned to leave and a man came in with a badge on that said sheriff. He didn't look much better than the deputy. He looked like he needed a bath too and his shirt was wrinkled and he needed a shave bad. He said, "What can I do for you?"

"I want to talk to you in private."

"You can talk in front of my deputy."

"I need to see you alone I that is Okay with you?"

The sheriff looked at the deputy and nodded his head toward the door. The deputy left but was saying something under his breath. When he left Jace said, "I need to know anything you can tell me about a man named Sam McMurtry."

The sheriff frowned, "Why do you want to know?"

"He has had some men killed and some were friends of mine and he had my girlfriend kidnaped and I want it to stop."

The sheriff replied, "You better leave Mr. McMurtry alone because he's a powerful man around here and I'd have to put you in jail if you bother him."

"Well sheriff I aim to bother him alright and if you want to put me in jail now is a good a time as any." His right hand touched his gun and the look he gave the sheriff he knew he better leave things alone.

"Hell I'll leave the problem to Mr. McMurtry."

"I figured you was on his payroll but I had to check anyway. Just stay out of our way and you won't get hurt."

Jace went outside and mounted his horse and they left town and waited just outside of town for Hank and Luther. They waited about an hour when they came riding up. Hank said, "We need to head southeast to his ranch. We are going to be his new hands."

Jace asked, "How did you arrange that?"

Hank laughed, "Of all things his foreman was there and said he liked us. Told us to be there early in the morning to go to work."

"Well we won't disappoint him we will be there. Lets ride toward his place and find a good place to make camp and talk about what we want to do."

They rode till they came to a nice large lake. They made camp and had dinner and talked. Hank said, "I don't think the foreman liked us so much as he was afraid of Luther."

They laughed, "I can't blame him. If he had to feed Luther he'd be more afraid."

Everyone laughed again. Luther said, "Well then feed me."

After they ate Jace said, "We will get an early start in the morning. I want to look the place over before daylight. If it is like I think it will be I want Luther and Steve to take the bunkhouse and don't let any of the hands out.. Hank you and Ray take the south side and Tim and Rick take the north side. We'll all go in at the same time. I will go in the house and get McMurtry and bring him outside."

"I don't think he is going to like that," Hank smiled.

"After all he has done I don't care what he likes. I plan to take care of this now no matter what it takes to get it done. He had my friends killed and kidnaped Jennifer so he better be happy if he comes out alive?"

"What if the sheriff warns him?"

"I don't think he will." Jace replied. " He was afraid I would shoot him and if he warns him I will come after him and he knows it. Lets get some sleep now and get an early start in the morning.."

Jace felt something was wrong and grabbed his six gun and hand it in Hanks face.

Hank said, "Sorry I just wanted to wake you it is two O'clock and I thought we better get started. "

"Sorry about that," Jace told him " " That is a good idea. Wake everyone else and lets eat and get going."

They ate a cold breakfast of jerky and water from the canteens. They rode till they were close to the ranch and Jace said, "Wait here and let me look over the next hill and see what is there. I think we are close now and I don't want to wander into a guard."

He got off and walked to the top and got down on his stomach and crawled the last few feet. He took off his hat and looked over the top. He saw a large ranch house and two barns behind that. To the right there was a long ranch house. That is where Luther and Steve would have to take care of the ranch hands. He went back and told everyone what he saw. He told Luther and Steve to circle around to the right and they would find the bunk house and he would go up the middle and get in the house. Tim and Rick would go left and Hank and Ray right

He said, "Watch out for night guards."

"We will and you watch your back," Tim replied.

Everyone left for their places. Jace walked to the top of the hill and crawled to a fence and went under it. Having not spotted anyone he went on to the porch of the house. He had no idea where to find their bedroom so he had to be very careful. He went inside and looked back to see if he could see anyone. He saw a mounted guard close to the bunkhouse and thought I hope Luther and Steve saw him. Well he thought I have to go on now no matter what happens now. He moved through the house and went up the stairs to the bedrooms. He saw a hall with six doors. He noticed the doors were all the same except one and it was larger and had fancy carving on it. That is the room of a powerful man he thought. He moved down the hall to that door. He was about to open it when he heard a noise. He flattened against the wall and didn't move. He saw a large woman come out of one of the rooms and go downstairs. He didn't know who she was. The cook should be downstairs someplace. When she had gone he eased the door open and eased inside. He saw two people under cover in the bed. He saw one had the cover on their head. That must be the wife so he went to the other side and saw a man. He slipped his gun out and put it to the mans head and cocked it. When he did the man jumped and reached for his gun. Jace clubbed his hand with his pistol and the man yelled.

Jace said, "If you want to live keep your mouth shut and I won't have to hurt you anymore.

"What do you want and who are you?" McMurtry asked.

"When we get down stairs I'll tell you all you need to know."

"Maybe you don't know who you 're messing with. I'm Sam McMurtry."

"I know who you are maybe you don't know who I am?"

He asked, "Who are you?"

"I'm Jace McCord."

The man turned pale and stated shaking. He asked, "What do you want?"

"You know why I am here. You sent enough men after me and had someone very special to me kidnaped. Just be glad they didn't hurt her."

"You won't get away with this McCord I will have the sheriff after you."

Jace laughed, "I met the sheriff do you really think I would worry about him?"

The mans wife was awake by now and she had the sheet pulled up around her. She looked like she might pass out.

"Don't worry Mam I am not going to hurt you. I think you have suffered enough just being married to this poor excuse for a man," Jace told her. "McMurtry get up and get dressed. Don't try anything because I'd like an excuse to shoot you and get this mess over with."

He got dressed and they went out to the front porch and Jace said, "Luther you and Steve bring the men out and lets talk to them."

They had them come out and Hank and Ray had two men with them. Jace said where did you get them. Ray said, "They were riding around guarding the place so we thought they would like to join us."

"Good you all come here and we are going to get this taken care of right now."

Luther and Steve brought the men from the bunk house and

Ray and Hank brought the two men they had and joined them by the porch.

Jace walked forward, "Men I am going to tell you all something and you better listen very carefully. I'm Jace McCord. Some of you may have heard of me?"

The men started talking among themselves. Most of them knew of Jace and didn't want anything to do with facing him.

Jace continued, "This boss of yours has sent a lot of men to kill me he had my girlfriend kidnaped. He has had some of my men killed. He has two boys in jail facing a murder trial and he doesn't like that so he tried to get them out by killing everyone that had anything keeping them in jail. He hit the town a couple of times and a few years ago had a sheriff and two deputies killed because they had his boys in jail for murder again. They are going to stand trail and will probably hang but that is the law and they are not above the law I don't care what their father thinks."

McMurtry said, "You won't get away with this."

Jace hit him in the mouth as hard as he could and said, "Shut up and listen for once in your life. I will face any one of you that wants to stop me."

One man said, "let me get my guns and I'll stop you."

A couple of the men said, "This is the shooter you can't go up against him."

"Give me my guns" the man said. I'll show you he ain't nothin but a loud mouth ass hole.

McMurtry said, "I will give you five thousand dollars if you take care of him."

"What about it you afraid to face me?" Jace said .

"Luther take him to the bunkhouse and let him get his guns."

They came back and the gunslinger looked like he knew how to use them.

"Hank come here and watch this man make sure he doesn't cause any trouble," Jace asked him.

He went out to the yard and faced the gunman. The man said, "When you're ready. "Jace didn't say anything.

The man said, "Go for your guns what are you yellow?"

Jace just stood there and watched the gunman. It was getting light enough to see his eyes. He saw the change in his eyes and went for his gun just as the other man went for his. Jace fired and the bullet hit him square in the chest. His gun fired in the ground and he sank down with a look like this is not happening. He fell to the ground and was still. Everyone was talking about how fast he was.

Even McMurtry was quiet. He said, "I never saw anyone move that fast before."

"You have two choices you can face me or you can accept the fact that your boys are going on trail for murder. If there was a way to prove it you would be on trial for murder with them but I don't know of any way to prove it."

McMurtry hung his head and cried like a baby. One of the men said, "Mr. McCord would you let us go if we promise not to cause you any trouble. We are just cowhands and want a job but not for this man."

"Any one of you that wants to leave has my permission but if you try anything I'll get you."

He said, "I promise we won't cause you any trouble."

McMurtry said, "If you all leave now you won't work around here anymore."

The foreman said, "I think you are the one that is through not us."

"Hank if you will get our bunch ready we can leave if a few minuets." Jace asked, "McMurtry if you wanted to come to the trail you can but you better not cause any trouble."

McMurtry's wife came out on the porch and asked, "Can I come to my boys trial?"

"Sure," Jace replied. "Ill promise no harm will come to you Ma'am."

She said, "I think I can show you how you can get the evidence against Sam. He turned my boys against me and they thought they could get away with anything. He is the reason they are on trial for murder."

McMurtry said, "You better keep your mouth shut or I will shut it for you for good."

Jace pulled his gun and put between McMurtry's eyes and said, "Shut your mouth because I have had all your big mouth I can take. I think you better let us take you somewhere safe Mrs McMurtry I think your life in danger now."

She said, "If you could take me to my brother's place about fifty miles from here he will take care of me."

"We sure will," Jace told her. "Ray and Rick would you get a buggy and hitch it for her?"

The foreman said "We'll do it for her she has always been good to us."

Jace said, "Ok that would be fine. Thanks men."

He turned to McMurtry and said, "If anything happens to your wife I'll come for you and you will face me want to or not."

The foreman ask Jace if him and a couple of the hands could ride with them to help Mrs McMurtry to her brothers.

Jace looked toward Mrs McMurtry and she nodded and Jace told the foreman, "I think that it would be fine if you men ride with us,"

They left McMurtry all alone. He had the dead gunslinger to keep him company. As they rode Jace came up beside the buggy and tied his horse behind and got in the rig with her. He asked, "How do you think you can prove he had anything to do with the killings?"

She said, "I kept some records that he didn't know about. They are at my brothers and they are safe. My brother would have gone after him long ago but he had so many men. We didn't know the men would not back him." Jace said "It was probably a good thing he didn't go after him."

"He is not the kind to give up. What about you he might try to get you?" Mrs. McMurtry asked.

"He's tried several times and failed. I think he is too afraid to try me."

Just then they heard a horse coming fast. Jace jumped off and pulled his rifle and saw McMurtry coming fast. He was shooting at anything he could.

Jace said, "The rest of you take the buggy and get out of here fast." He turned and watched him coming at him. He waited till he got in range and felt something tug at his sleeve. He aimed and fired. McMurtry hit the ground and Jace ran to check him. He was barely alive when he got there.

"How did you get away from me I had so many men trying to kill you?"

Jace said, "You needed better men I guess."

As he died Jace said, "Well I guess we can bury you before we leave."

Just then Hank and Rick rode up and Luther and Steve had Mrs. McMurtry in her buggy. She put her hands to her face and cried. She had several years of grief to get rid of. Tim said, "Jace I hear riders coming."

"Get in front of the buggy in case it is trouble."

They all took positions in front and pulled their rifles. They watched as the riders came closer. None of them had any guns pulled so Jace said, "Easy they don't seem to want a fight."

"It is the men from the ranch," Rick said.

Jace went to meet them. One of the men spoke, "We saw him take off and we thought we better follow."

"Well I had to kill him," Jace told the men.

One of the men got off and put out his hand, "My name is Sam Stover cowboy of the bar eight ranch or should I say the former ranch."

Jace shook his hand, "Thank all you men."

He heard Mrs. McMurtry say, "If you would stay I would like to keep you all on as hands and Jim I can't think of a better foreman."

"Yes Ma'am I sure would stay and help you. I think I speak for the rest of the boys too." They all said, "We all would like to stay, you were always good to us and we will help any way we can."

She said, "Mr. McCord I think I will stay here and send word to my brother. He can come and help me get started again."

"I think you will be fine now. Looks like you have a good crew to help you."

"If you ever come this way again I hope you will come by and visit us," She told Jace.

"Sure will. Bye."

They were all ready to get back to Hays and see everyone. They sent a telegram at the first place they could and rode hard the rest of the way home.

It was early afternoon when they arrived in Hays. A young boy ran down the street yelling they are back they are back. Fred came out of his office and waved at them. Jennifer ran out and jumped to Jace and he pulled her up and kissed her. They got down and he held her close and told her everything will be all right now. The rest of the girls ran to meet them and they all hugged and kissed and cried.

Jace told Jennifer to look at Luther he had Hailey up and she was a long way from the ground. She kissed him and he turned red because every one was watching. They laughed and took the horses to the livery. Fred said "I want everyone to come to our house tonight for dinner."

Steve started to walk away and Fred said, "Can you come too?"

Steve said, "You mean you want me too?"

They all said, "You're one of us now." Jace thought for a minute he would cry. He said, "I ain't never had no one treat me like you folks do."

"You are a good man to have at your back in a fight and that is something to be happy about," Jace told him.

Fred Lawson came up and told Steve, "Son you helped all the people in this town and rode with the men that went after my daughter when she had been kidnaped and when the went after McMurtry. You have a place here and friends as long as you want."

Steve turned and wiped his eyes and said "I ain't never been this happy."

They all met for dinner and had a good time laughing and eating. After dinner while the girls cleaned the kitchen they went to the front porch. Fred asked, "What all happened?"

Jace told him the story about killing the man and his wife having the ranch hands wanting to help her.

"I sure am glad that is over," Fred said. "I spent everyday telling the girls that you were all Okay."

They talked a while and the girls came out and sat with them. Jace said, "While you are all here I want to tell you something. I have a place in northern New Mexico and I would like to go there and build a heard back and run that ranch."

They all tried to talk at once. He said "I don't know how to say what I have got to tell you. I don't want to do something that might cause any of you to do something that you don't want to do. Well here goes. I know this is not a good time and not very romantic but I want to ask Jennifer to marry me and go with me."

She grabbed him and kissed him and said, "Yes, yes, I will marry you anytime you say."

"I want to tell the rest of you I have never had better friends than you all. I want any of you that would like to, to help me build the ranch and run it."

They all tried to talk at once and Fred spoke. He said, "I knew one day I would loose one of my girls but I think I am going to loose both of them. I couldn't be happier though. I think they have chosen well and I also think I am going to loose a secretary."

Luther tried to say something but couldn't say it. Hailey said, "When he gets ready I will say yes." Everyone laughed and were very happy.

Watch for next book "Jace in New Mexico"

Printed in the United States
45926LVS00002B/319-366